KILL BALL

I0629321

CARLTON MELLICK III

ERASERHEAD PRESS
PORTLAND, OREGON

ERASERHEAD PRESS
205 NE BRYANT
PORTLAND, OR 97211

WWW.ERASERHEADPRESS.COM

ISBN: 1-62105-053-X

AUTHOR'S NOTE

Did you ever see that movie *Bubble Boy* that came out in 2001? Yeah, the one Disney released that was kind of like *The Boy in the Plastic Bubble* with wacky slapstick comedy. What the fuck was up with that movie? Whose brilliant idea was it to turn a horrifying disability into something cute and fun, where the bubble boy is basically just a super bouncy ball with legs? Really, I want to know who, because that man is a fucking genius. I want to shake his hand. I don't care about whether it was a good movie or not, or whether it was offensive to those suffering from bubble boy disease or not. I just care that it exists. Because it just *has* to exist. There are some stories that must be told no matter how stupid the concept, for example *Time Cop* or *The Kobold Wizard's Dildo of Enlightenment +2 (an adventure for 3-6 players, levels 2-5)*.

When I first came up with the idea for *Kill Ball*, it was a much different story than it ended up being. Originally, it was supposed to be set in the real world and was going to be about a mafia hitman with bubble boy disease. I was picturing a Harvey Keitel-esque hired killer with a stone-cold expression on his face, walking down an alley in a man-sized bulletproof hamster ball as if it weren't the most ridiculous thing anyone has ever seen. He would not have been a wacky super bouncy ball like Bubble Boy. He would have been an unstoppable killing machine, who would assassinate people by smashing them against walls or rolling over them. It would have been hilarious.

But I also had another story I wanted to write called *The Girl with the Hairspray Eyes*, which was meant to be a parody of 1970s Italian thrillers (like those by the masterful Dario Argento) set in a world where everyone lives inside of plastic bubbles—kind of like an apocalyptic version of Bubble Boy with a serial killer on the loose. Since only one bizarro bubble boy book needs to exist in this world, I had to choose between the two concepts. I decided to go with the concept for The Girl with the Hairspray Eyes (but still use the Kill Ball title) because there was much more I could do with this concept. Maybe I'll use the hitman in the plastic bubble for something else at a later date.

As I have said in previous books, my favorite way to write a story is to take an incredibly ridiculous idea and approach it with complete sincerity. Kill Ball is such a book. It is set in a world that is too absurd to possibly exist. It is especially absurd that everyone chose to roll around in plastic balls instead of wearing spacesuits, which would have been the more logical thing to do. But let's forget about that. The concept of bubble people is far more interesting and terrifying than spacesuit people. I imagine it being like a real world version of Weeble World, where weebles wobble but they don't fall down.

But the funniest part of this concept is that it's basically a tongue-in-cheek parody of 1970s Italian slasher thrillers. It contains the classic trope of these films—the unseen killer holding a knife in his black leather gloves. Only within this book, the murderer is in a black leather bubble that has a knife sticking out of it.

Kind of like this:

Now I'm not sure if that's the scariest or dumbest killer anyone's ever come up with for a slasher story. Most likely it is both. In any case, the second I came up with this idea there was no way that I could possibly not write it. So that's what I did. And here it is.

I'm proud to present to you my 37th book. I hope you enjoy it as much as I enjoyed writing it.

—Carlton Mellick III, 9/27/2012 4:01 pm

CHAPTER ONE

All Colin Hinchcliff ever wanted as a child was to hug his mother. But this was something he could never do. It wasn't allowed.

"It's dangerous to touch her," his father always told him. "No matter what you do you should never, ever touch her."

But Colin was only four years old. He didn't understand why his mother lived inside of a plastic bubble. He didn't understand why he wasn't allowed to be in there with her.

"You'll understand when you're older, Puppydog," his father said.

Puppydog was what his father always called him.

Colin would often try to hug his mother through the plastic barrier that separated them, but it just wasn't the same as when he hugged his father or grandmother. It just felt like he was hugging a rubber raft or a big human-shaped beach ball. He couldn't feel even a single degree of her body warmth through the plastic.

It just wasn't enough for him. He wanted her to hold him tightly in her arms, kiss him on the forehead, and press her cheek against his cheek as she did so long ago in the early days of his life that only his instincts remembered. So he decided to break the rules.

When she was taking a nap one languid Sunday afternoon, Colin tried to open the seal to his mother's plastic bubble. But the entrance was locked and child-proofed. No matter how hard he pulled on the rubbery handle, he could not get it open. Colin had to open it another way.

He remembered how his father carved a smiling face into a pumpkin for Halloween the week before. Colin wondered if he could use the same tools to carve a passageway through the plastic barrier to get to his mother.

"Whatcha doing, Puppydog?" his father asked from the living room, yelling over the blaring sound of the football game on television.

"Nothing," Colin said, as he opened the pantry to get to the garbage bag.

The football game was so loud that his father couldn't hear Colin as he rummaged through the trash. It wasn't long before the boy spotted the orange handle of the disposable cutting device.

"Why don't you come in here and watch the game with me?" his father called from the other room.

"No, thanks," Colin said, standing outside his mother's bubble.

He pressed the serrated blade into the plastic wall using all his strength until it punctured through. Then, just as his father carved a long nose-shaped hole in his pumpkin, he sawed downward.

"Don't bother your mother in there," called his father. "She's trying to sleep."

The slit in the plastic ran all the way to the carpeting by the time Colin was finished cutting.

"I won't," Colin said.

A strong, pleasant smell filled his runny nostrils as he crawled through the plastic. It was a familiar smell, reminiscent of dandelions and baked plums. It was a smell that he had completely forgotten about until that very moment. It was the smell of his mother.

When he saw his mother, it was as if he was seeing her for the first time. She looked different than he imagined. She wasn't as blurry as she appeared through the plastic wall. She looked just as human as his father.

He just watched her for a while as she lay in her big cozy bed, deep inside of a comfortable dream. When she opened her eyes, Colin smiled at her.

"Mommy?" he said.

She shot up from the bed, tossing her covers away and stared back at him like he was a miniature devil creeping toward her.

She looked angry. Colin knew he was going to get into trouble for this, but he didn't care. Before she could yell at him, he ran at her and wrapped his arms around her hips. She tried to push him away, but he held her with all of his strength.

"Don't be mad," Colin cried. "I just want to be in here with you."

His mother pushed against him.

"Please don't make me go away," he said, refusing to let go. "Please. Just let me stay a little while."

His mother stopped resisting. Her muscles relaxed. Then she hugged him back, holding him gently in her arms.

"Fine," she said, her voice soft and calming. "You can stay in here just this once. Just for a little while."

As they embraced, Colin felt his mother's tears wet his cheeks. She stroked his hair and kissed his forehead so hard it nearly gave him whiplash.

"It's okay," his mother said. "Everything will be fine."

Colin closed his eyes and relished the moment. He couldn't believe he was finally able to hug his mother without plastic between them. It was a moment he would remember for the rest of his life.

When his father got up to get another beer, he came across the orange-handled blade on the floor, then noticed the tear in the plastic barrier, then saw his son in the one place he was forbidden to enter.

"What the hell are you doing?" his father screamed at him. "You fucking idiot!"

Colin panicked, he held his mother tighter.

He looked up at her and said, "I don't want to leave. Don't make me leave."

"Don't worry," she said, water pouring from her eyes. "It's not your fault."

"Get out of there!" his father screamed from outside of the bubble. "Get the fuck out of there now!"

The tears flowing out of his mother's eyes became thick, thicker than the texture of normal tears. The color of the fluid darkened to a shade of pink, creamy like milk.

"Mommy?" Colin said.

The smile faded from her face as her eyeballs dripped out of their sockets like runny egg whites.

"Mommy!" Colin cried, hugging her and shaking her arms.

"Quickly," his father yelled, tugging on the plastic exterior. "Get out of there now! Get away from her!"

The skin on her face loosened and slipped down her neck onto her pajamas.

"I'm sorry," Colin cried to his mother. "I didn't mean to come in. I'm sorry!"

Her hair slid off, revealing a gooey skull.

"It's okay," his mother said, teeth falling out of her lipless mouth like soggy pieces of candy corn. "You didn't know any better."

"I'm sorry!" Colin said, holding her hands, scared to let go.

His father opened the entrance of the plastic bubble and ran inside. He grabbed Colin by the waist.

"I said get away from her you little shit!" his father said as he dragged his son away from his mother.

Outside of the plastic barrier, his father smacked him across the face so hard that blood sprayed out of his nose and lips at the same time.

"I told you never to go in there," screamed his father, pointing Colin's eyes in the direction of his mother. "Now look at what you did. Look at what you did to your mother!"

Colin was forced to watch as his mother's body fell apart. She became soggy. She was turning into liquid.

"It's all your fault," his father said, slapping his son again. "You killed her." His eyes became red with tears. His voice cracked between sobs. "Why didn't you listen to me? Why?"

Colin just said that he was sorry over and over again, as if apologizing enough would put her back to normal. It wasn't until his mother was just a fizzling puddle on the ground that he realized there was no undoing what he had done.

"She said it wasn't my fault," Colin said.

It was all he could think of to say.

From that day on, he was without his mother.

And his father never called him Puppydog ever again.

At first, only a small percentage of the population was infected with the disease that killed Colin's mother. But the epidemic spread quickly. It wasn't long before Colin and his father were also behind plastic walls.

The virus spared not a single human being. By the time Colin started grade school, everyone in the world lived inside of plastic bubbles. And then the world became a very different place.

Colin was still too young to understand much about the disease. All he knew was that if he ever left his bubble he would melt away just like his mother did. And he would never be able to touch another human being with his own hands again. He would never be able to have a wife that he could lie with or have children he could give piggyback rides to. From that point on, humans would only reproduce through a very tricky method of artificial insemination.

But this was not something Colin was able to deal with. The older he became, the more he craved physical human contact. Just being able to hold somebody's hand would have been enough. The counselors told him he would learn to live with it like everyone else. But he didn't learn. Things only got worse.

CHAPTER TWO

The streets were filled with hundreds of rolling human heads the size of tractor tires. That was how Colin saw human beings these days: as giant rolling heads. It was because of how human culture had adapted since the epidemic.

"Out of the way, Eightball!" said an angry rolling head as it slammed into the back of Colin's plastic bubble.

Colin moved out of the way and let the angry head roll past him down the sidewalk.

"Sorry," Colin said.

The plastic bubbles they occupied were similar to hamster balls—those little plastic spherical cages that hamsters and gerbils used to run around in decades ago—but large enough to fit human beings. It was the way people got around when they weren't inside of their homes. But unlike hamster balls, you couldn't see the humans inside the plastic. You could only see their giant faces, which were printed across the entire surface of the bubbles. It made them look like rolling heads.

Colin pushed on the inner side of his ball to get back on the rubber sidewalk. And then he moved forward, rolling along like a giant hamster crossing a living room.

"Hey Eightball, nice clothes!" somebody yelled from a freckle-faced bubble next to him.

Colin tried to ignore the guy. He was used to getting picked on for his clothes.

People didn't actually wear clothes anymore, at least not the kind made of fabric that used to be so commonplace. Because the plastic bubbles offered all the warmth and protection one could need, everyone went around naked inside of their balls. What people referred to as *clothing* was the exterior of a person's plastic bubble.

"Trying to be ironic or something?" said the freckle-head, following Colin down the rubber road. He obviously had nothing better to do.

In the beginning, people would just color the outside of their balls orange or blue. Like tinted windows, they could see out of their plastic bubbles but nobody could see their naked bodies within. But then the fashion industry stepped in and created all kinds of styles and patterns to liven up the exterior of people's bubbles. Some people had checkered bubbles, some had polka dot bubbles, and some had striped Easter egg bubbles. Then bubbles were decorated to look like globes of the Earth or other planets, and then decorated with paintings by famous artists like Salvador Dali or Jackson Pollock. Eventually it became a trend to decorate the outside of your bubble with a picture of your own face.

"Why aren't you wearing a picture of your face?" said freckle-head. Colin watched his giant face as he spoke, even though the mouth didn't move. "Do you think looking like an eightball is cool or something?"

Colin turned his eightball-patterned bubble at the punk.

"I used to play pool professionally," Colin said. "I don't care about dumb fashion trends. These are the only clothes that suit me."

"Well, it looks stupid," said freckle-head, bonking his bubble against Colin's as if trying to start a fight.

Colin slammed him right back and sent freckle-head flying across the street, spinning in circles. The punk should have known not to mess with an eightball.

Colin rolled up a ramp into a subway car. A beeping noise sounded as he passed through the door, signaling that his bank account had just been charged the ticket fare.

"Six seventy-five?" Colin asked, as he looked at the receipt that popped up on his wrist computer. "They raised the price again?"

He grumbled to himself as he rolled down the aisle toward an open seat.

"They could charge us anything they want," said a pink-haired bubble-head behind him. "It's not like we have any other transportation options."

An old gray-haired bubble-head in front of him said, "I miss being able to drive cars." Her giant upside-down face stared blankly at Colin, then rotated upward as she walked. "It used to be so much easier to get around in the old days."

"What kind of car did you drive?" asked pink-hair. "I never had one."

"Oh, I don't remember exactly," said gray-hair. "But it was red and really cute!"

Colin realized he had created a conversation and was right in the middle of it. When he took his seat, he ended up getting stuck between them.

"I wish I got to drive a car before they were outlawed," said pink-hair, rolling into the seat next to Colin's.

They weren't exactly seats, more like holes in the floor that kept the plastic bubbles from rolling around. When all the passengers were situated, the subway car looked like a carton of eggs.

"It seems everything's getting outlawed these days," said gray-hair, her giant bubble face pointed at the ceiling.

"I know!" said pink-hair. "Can you believe the curfew they ordered last night? They're even trying to outlaw staying out late!"

"Oh, I don't blame them for that one," said gray-hair. "There's a madman on the loose. I wouldn't be staying out too late even if there wasn't a curfew in effect."

"How many victims have there been so far?"

"Ten. All women."

"It's terrifying."

Pink-hair's bubble shuddered against Colin's.

Colin tried to imagine what the women looked like inside

of their bubbles. The images of their faces on their exteriors didn't give him much of an idea. As hard as he tried, he couldn't visualize them. To him, they were just giant rolling heads with no expression on their faces.

"But we have nothing to worry about," said gray-hair. "The killer's only been targeting low-life women. You know, *those* types."

"But still!"

"They should just have all of *those* places shut down anyway. They're so disgusting."

Colin suddenly felt uncomfortable sitting between them, since he was actually headed to one of *those* places at that very moment.

"Men are such pigs."

"Obviously the killer is a man. It seems men are snapping a lot lately. Because sex has become impossible, they're all going insane with sexual frustration."

"They masturbate constantly."

Colin felt even more uncomfortable sitting between them.

"I bet every man on this train is masturbating right now," said gray-hair.

"They should outlaw public masturbation. Even if we can't see them inside their balls, it's still disgusting."

Human beings had not been able to touch each other for almost thirty years, and many people had become mentally unstable because of it. But it wasn't only the lack of touch that was a problem. Ever since people started covering up their bubble exterior with *clothes* they had not been able to see each other, either. The only way humans made any kind of connection anymore was through voice. And because Colin didn't really like to speak all that much, he felt especially cut off from humanity.

He was trapped, imprisoned, isolated, and though he was surrounded by dozens of people on the subway train he couldn't have felt more alone.

There was only one place Colin could go that would ease his frustration and make him feel sane again. It was when he went to one of *those* places—the kind of place many people liked to pretend no longer existed.

She was like a mermaid swimming through the air as she danced on the stage of the strip club, sliding her naked body against the inside of her plastic bubble. A goddess with purple peacock hair, swirling turquoise-colored tattoos, and big blue eyes that pierced through every man they gazed upon.

As Colin watched her through his black eightball bubble, his eyes were tearing up from the lack of blinking.

The strip club was the only place left in the world where Colin could see another human being. Erotic dancers didn't wear clothes on the exterior of their bubbles, so he went to these places to remind himself of what human beings actually looked like inside their balls. He had no idea he would end up falling in love with one of the dancers.

In the dimly lit club, Colin was surrounded by giant head-shaped balls. All of them were faces of men, jiggling up and down. It was always obvious when a guy was masturbating inside of his bubble, because his head would jiggle up and down.

Over the last thirty years, strip clubs had become the ultimate sexual taboo. Even though they were in ways less seedy than they had been in the past, they were abhorred more than ever because they were the last remnant of human sexuality left in the culture.

"Want a private dance?" said a soft female voice.

He turned to see a naked woman pressing her translucent bubble against his. She had black curly hair, dark skin, and big white circles tattooed on her cheeks that gave her an almost clownish look.

"You know you do," she said, pressing her large breasts against his plastic barrier.

Her nipples were erect enough to pop through her bubble and kill them both.

"No thanks," Colin said.

He was always approached by women when he came to these clubs, probably because his faceless ball seemed safer and nonthreatening. Also, he was never masturbating while watching the girls.

"Suit yourself," said the woman, rolling her translucent ball to the next customer.

Colin only cared about one woman in the club. It was the one on stage at that moment: Siren, the mermaid of the sexual sea.

Even though she was not dressed like a mermaid, that's how everyone saw her. It was because of how she danced. She would grease her body up with a shiny lubricant and swim inside of her plastic ball like a fish in a bowl, gliding against the sides as it rolled around the stage. She was acrobatic in an almost magical way. They say she was once a part of a new age circus that went out of business a few years ago.

When he watched Siren, it was the only time he could forget that he was trapped inside of a plastic ball. Her eyes seemed to suck his soul out of his body, out of his bubble, luring him across the room toward her. It made him feel alive and free. It was the reason he continued coming back, every night, spending all the money that he could spare.

"You're back again?" Siren asked him, as she rolled through the club between sets.

"Yeah," Colin said.

He was awkward. When she looked at him through his bubble, it was as though she could see him inside of there. Her eyes always connected with his eyes. It made him feel naked and helpless.

"You are the same eightball who keeps coming in every night, right?"

"Yes," Colin said.

She rolled her ball up to his, pressing them together as if embracing his arm.

"I like that you have your own style," she said, touching his eightball clothing through her plastic. "It's really unique."

"Well, it used to be my uniform," Colin said.

"Uniform?"

"I was a professional pool player back when it was a popular sport."

"Cool," she said, not genuinely interested. "Want a dance?"

Colin knew he shouldn't, but he couldn't resist.

"Sure," he said.

She smiled at him with bright red lips. As Colin gazed into her eyes and admired her wild blue and purple makeup, she winked. A flirtatious butterfly wink. Colin swore she was winking directly at him.

Inside a private booth, Siren rolled him into a corner, squeezing his bubble against the wall. They called it a lap dance, but it wasn't exactly a dance and had nothing to do with laps. It was where the dancer rubbed her body against the client through the plastic, usually to the rhythm of a song.

"So what's pool like?" Siren said, while waiting for the song to come begin. "I've never heard of it before."

The sound of his bank account being charged a large sum of money beeped on his wrist computer. As per the deal, for every moment Colin spent in her presence, Siren would drain his account like a vampire.

"A contact sport," Colin said. "It was based on an ancient game where people hit balls into holes."

When the song started, an old techno song, Siren slithered like an eel against Colin's bubble.

Out of awkwardness, Colin continued, "Only in this sport the humans were the balls and they played on a court instead

20

of a table. The object of the game was to knock the opposing team members into the holes."

She turned around and rolled her butt against Colin's upper thighs, kneading it against him.

When she rose up and pressed her back against Colin's chest, she said, "Were you any good?"

The material of the dancers' bubbles was much thinner than other bubbles, so Colin could almost feel the warmth of her body through the plastic. He wished his bubble was made of the same material, so he could feel even more of her.

"Only star players got the position of eightball," Colin said. "I was the best."

When Colin felt his penis become erect, Siren did not pull away from him as most dancers would. Instead, she massaged it with her stomach like a belly dancer.

"It's too bad nobody plays it anymore," he said.

As she danced against him with her belly, she looked up at Colin with her bright eyes. It was still as if she could see him through his black ball, looking him directly in the eyes.

Then Colin felt something unusual. It was just his imagination, but it felt as if her hands were entering Colin's bubble and wrapping around him. He could feel the warmth of her hands around him, the tightness of her fingers as they squeezed his naked ass. It was all in his imagination. It had to be. But Colin closed his eyes and allowed the hallucination to take over him.

He felt her squeeze his ass tighter, then pull him toward her, pulling him all the way into her bubble. She wrapped herself around him, slithering their bodies together. It felt as if she had a hundred limbs rubbing against him.

Then the song was over and she pulled away, pushing Colin back into his own bubble. When he opened his eyes, she was staring back at him. A smile on her face.

"You're magical," Colin told her.

But she was already rolling out of the private room, heading for the side stage. She looked back at him only once with a smug expression on her face, as if she knew she had him. She knew he wouldn't be able to resist coming back for more.

Colin stayed until Siren's very last dance of the night. But even that wasn't enough. He had to see her one last time. Outside of the club, in the alley out back, he waited for her behind the dumpsters. It was where he waited for her every night, trying to gather up the courage to speak with her.

He knew he wouldn't be able to see the real Siren as she left the club. She would have switched bubbles with one that was clothed, that he wouldn't be able to see through. But he would still get to see the inflated picture of her face. He would still be able to imagine what she looked like inside of there.

That night he vowed to say something/anything to her. It didn't matter what. If she didn't fall in love with him soon, he didn't know what he was going to do. Going to the club every night was getting to be too expensive.

When he heard the back door of the club open, he peeked out to see who it was. It wasn't Siren. It was just a worker drone.

The giant spider-shaped machine crawled across the alley toward the dumpster. It had a big white cartoon smiley face on the center of its black ball body. Eight multi-purpose limbs grew out of its side, clacking as it walked on the rubber walkway, dragging a bag of trash with its fine metal webbing. The drone made clicking noises against the metal as it climbed the dumpster and tossed the trash within.

"Hello, want to see me dance?" said the robotic spider.

Colin noticed the drone was looking down at him from the top of the dumpster, staring at him with its cartoon smile. It was talking to him.

"Hello, want to see me dance?" repeated the spider.

Its voice was high-pitched yet monotone. The voice was

purposely designed to sound robotic yet cute.

Colin hated this model of drone. The point of drones was to have them do tasks that humans were not able to do outside of their bubbles. They were meant to be efficient and obedient. But for some reason the company that made this model of drone decided to give it personality. These drones were programmed to do all kinds of random pointless crap for the sake of entertainment.

"Hello, want to see me dance?" repeated the spider.

It wasn't going to shut up. If Colin didn't get rid of it the thing would give away his hiding spot and ruin everything.

"Go away," Colin told it. "I don't want to see your stupid dance."

The spider paused, sitting on top of the dumpster.

It smiled down on him for a few minutes.

Then it said, "Are you sure you don't want to see me dance?"

"I'm positive," Colin said. "Please leave me alone."

The spider continued smiling.

"I think you'll really like my dance," said the spider.

Colin wanted to strangle the robot.

"Fine," Colin said. "Do your stupid dance."

The spider crawled down from the dumpster into the middle of the alley. Then it turned in a circle to face Colin. Loud wacky dance music started playing and the spider did a bouncy hopping dance, spinning its smiling face in circles, and raising its spindly limbs in the air as if it were raising the roof.

Colin squeezed into the back corner behind the dumpster, positive the loud music and dancing robot would give him away. He cursed himself for not smashing the thing against the wall.

The door opened and somebody stepped out.

"Shut up, stupid wocko," said a woman's voice.

Wocko-bots. That's what the spider drones were called. It went immediately silent upon the woman's command.

Colin peeked out from behind the dumpster to see the

woman was Siren. She was now in her street clothes. Her giant ball-shaped head rolled out of the club into the alleyway.

"Get back inside," she told the wocko-bot.

The wocko-bot slunk downward and stepped slowly back into the club.

"He wanted to see my dance," said the wocko-bot as it disappeared into the building.

Upon hearing its words, Siren froze. Then her inflated head turned to see the eightball hiding in the shadows. Colin had been found out. He didn't know what to do. His plan had backfired.

"Hi," Colin said, rolling out from his hiding spot.

He wasn't sure what to say. He hoped that she would have something to say to him. He hoped she would be happy to see him.

"It's me," Colin said. "The pro pool player from earlier. You gave me a lap dance."

Siren's head rolled backward, as if she were looking straight up in the air, ignoring him.

"I've been coming to see you every day for months," Colin said. "You've given me seventeen lap dances so far. Don't you remember?"

The woman rolled further away from him, not able to say a word.

"I thought it was about time we spoke outside of the club," he said. "There's a million things I want to tell you."

When he rolled toward her, she screamed.

"Franko," she cried. "Franko, get out here now!"

"What's wrong?" Colin asked. "Are you okay?"

A large ball slammed out of the back door. It was the face of a hefty bald man.

"What's going on?" said the fat-head. "Is this guy bugging you?"

He was obviously one of the bouncers. He rolled in front of Colin, blocking his path to the dancer.

"I just want to talk to her," Colin said. "I'm not some creep. She knows me."

"That true?" Franko asked.

"I have no idea who he is," Siren said.

"Why don't you get out of here," said the bouncer. "I'll take care of this guy."

Without a word, Siren's big inflated head rolled away as fast as it could go. Colin tried to roll around the man in his path, but he wouldn't get out of his way.

"Get lost, creep," said the bouncer.

"I'm not a creep," Colin said. "You don't understand. This is important."

"Go home," Franko said. "You're scaring the girl."

Colin knew he could slam the guy out of the way if he wanted to, no matter how big he was inside his ball. He was a star eightball. He was a pro. But he didn't want to piss the bouncer off. He didn't want to get banned from the club.

"Fine," Colin said, rolling away.

"Don't ever try anything like this ever again," Franko said. "Or I'll break your neck."

"I won't," Colin said.

The bouncer followed him around to the front of the club, making sure he went in the opposite direction and didn't try to go after her.

But Colin wasn't worried about losing her. He knew where she lived. He had been following her home every night for the past two weeks.

CHAPTER THREE

Colin took the shortcut down the railslide, which was a downhill walkway similar to a roller coaster. You just rolled your plastic bubble into the tube and it shot you like a pinball across town. With this, Colin would be able to catch up to Siren in no time.

"Better hurry home," said the gate attendant, his wide beard-ed face filling up the entire ticket booth. "Curfew goes into effect in twenty minutes."

"Already?" Colin asked.

"It's a thousand dollar fine," said the attendant. "And you don't even have to be caught by a policeman, either. If you're out on the streets even one second past curfew, your bank account will automatically be charged a thousand dollars per hour until you're back indoors."

"What if I don't have a thousand dollars in my account?" Colin asked.

"Then your name goes on the wanted list," said the attendant.

"That's hardly fair."

"It's the law. There's nothing you can do about it."

Then a spider drone squirted green fluid through Colin's ventilation shaft, splashing him in the face.

"Have a good day," said the attendant, as he let Colin through.

Colin was too busy rubbing the greasy liquid all over his naked body to return the attendant's social nicety. It was mandatory to use a hefty amount of lubricant before going on the railslide or the friction burns would rub your skin bloody. Colin was always paranoid of friction burns.

While he shot across the city, rolling through loops and around buildings, he wondered how he was going to get off the streets before curfew. Siren and Colin lived on different sides of town. There was no way he could get to her, have a nice chat, then get back home before his account was charged.

There was only one solution. He had to convince Siren to let him stay the night at her place. If he could make her fall in love with him, it would be easy. The only problem was that he had to accomplish this within the next twenty minutes.

"I'll beat you home, my love," Colin said, as he rolled up the railslide tube. "Once you understand how I feel about you, I'm sure you'll want to be with me forever."

When he saw Siren again, he cut her off in the middle of the rubber street. The curfew was only a few minutes away, so nobody else was around. Nobody else would get in his way this time.

Siren's giant head froze in place when she saw Colin roll into the street in front of her, the number eight pointed in her direction.

"It's me," he said. "Colin. Remember?"

She rolled slowly backward.

"Don't go," he said. "There's a curfew."

"What do you want?" she said.

Her voice was frantic. Colin didn't really understand why.

"I just want to talk with you," Colin said. "I think you're so amazing."

He moved forward and she moved back.

"Get away from me," she cried.

"Can I spend the night at your place?" he asked. "If you don't have a guest room, I'll stay inside my travel bubble."

She picked up her pace, rolling in the opposite direction.

"Where are you going?" he asked. "Your home is the other way."

She kept running, speeding off into the distance. Colin chased after her. He realized she didn't understand what he was trying to say to her. He had to catch up to her and make sure she knew just how much he cared about her.

As he followed her down the street, he wondered what it would be like to marry Siren. He hoped it would be like having his own private dancer, who would perform for him nightly in the center of his living room. And then he could always see her real human form, any time he wanted, for the rest of his life.

"There's a man chasing me," said the woman. "I think he's the serial murderer that's been on the news."

Colin heard her as he rolled down the street. The dancer was around the corner, hiding from him. She had the police on the line.

"My name's Shanya James," she said as quietly as she could into her wrist computer. "What? Yes, I work at Luscious Ladies."

Colin could hear the operator's voice on the other line, but couldn't hear what was being said.

"Yes, his bubble is all black," she said. "He's a regular at the club. He looks like an eightball."

Colin rolled up to the corner, listening to the conversation. He thought it would be rude to interrupt her, so he waited patiently until she was finished.

"Stay here?" she said. "I don't have time to wait for the cop balls. He's after me!"

Colin didn't want the cops showing up. They would get in the way. And curfew was just about to begin.

"Hello?" the woman said. "Are you there?"

The voice on the other end was silent.

"I can't hear you," she said. She hung up and dialed again. "Hello? Hello? Shit!"

She couldn't get the police back on the phone.

Colin prepared to turn the corner and confront her, but he thought it might be better to first figure out what he was going to say. He wasn't much of a talker, though. He didn't have a lot of practice translating his thoughts and feelings into words.

Telling her that he loved her just wasn't enough. Perhaps if she knew more about him she might be less afraid. He wished she could see how athletic he was within his bubble. He wished she knew everything about him, especially how much time and money he has spent going to see her. That would have to be his plan. He would turn the corner and tell her exactly how much of his hard-earned money has been transferred from his bank account to hers. Colin was sure that would get her attention.

By the time Colin turned the corner, Siren was already a couple of blocks away, rolling quietly through the alley. He decided to roll casually after her. He didn't want to charge her. That would give her the wrong impression. He didn't want to come off as too desperate.

Halfway down the alleyway, something merged between them. It was somebody else. Somebody in a plastic bubble.

Colin paused. At first, he was worried that it was a cop ball come to arrest him for breaking curfew without money in his account. But it didn't look at all like a cop ball.

The bubble was not decorated with a human face as most balls were. This one was all black, like Colin's. But it wasn't an eightball. Its exterior was made of black leather.

Colin realized the person within the bubble hadn't noticed him yet. The black leather ball rolled quietly after Siren, keeping up with her pace. Colin crept quietly after the black ball.

Who was it? Colin had to find out. He had to know if he had a rival who was also pursuing Siren romantically. Colin was not very good at communicating with other people, especially women. He didn't know if he could compete with another suitor.

He debated giving up and turning around. When he was

a sportsman, he was all about competition. But with women he was easily discouraged. He had never had a girlfriend in his life. Even though relationships could not go much further than chatting, spending time together, and maybe rubbing up against each other's plastic barriers, Colin still always wanted to find somebody to love.

The moment Colin turned around to leave, a flash of movement grabbed his attention. The black ball sped up, charging Siren.

"Look out!" Colin yelled, but she was too far away to hear him.

She cried for help when she saw the black ball coming at her.

Colin didn't know what the heck was going on, but he knew he had to do something. He rolled down the alleyway as fast as he could to catch up.

A razor sharp blade emerged from the side of the black leather bubble, pointed at Siren. She screamed at the sight of the weapon as it spun in circles.

"Run," Colin yelled. "Get out of there!"

He tried to call the police on his wrist computer, but the call wouldn't connect. A note on his monitor said that the signal was out of range.

"That's impossible," Colin said. The signal was never out of range.

When the man in the black ball collided with Siren, he rammed her against the wall knife-first. It pierced through the plastic, popping her bubble.

"No!" Colin screamed.

But it was too late. The blade was driven deep into the woman's chest.

Colin froze. He dropped to his knees within his bubble, sitting down on his greasy ankles.

The black ball turned slowly in Colin's direction. He couldn't see his face, but Colin knew the man was staring at him. Challenging him to take revenge.

"You murderer," Colin whimpered. "I'll kill you, you murderer."

It was all he could say.

When the man in the black ball was sure that Colin was just going to lie there and do nothing, he flipped his blade back into his bubble with a *shwishing* sound. Then he slowly turned and rolled in the other direction.

Colin walked somberly toward the dead body, to say goodbye to his love. He didn't care about the curfew fine. He didn't really care about anything anymore.

"I'm sorry I didn't save you," Colin said, rolling like a snail. "I'm such an idiot. All this time I've been trying to tell you how much you mean to me, yet when it came time to actually prove it I just stood there. I failed you."

Then he looked down at her.

"Could you ever forgive me?" he asked the body as it became water and ooze on the rubber walkway.

But then he noticed something funny about the corpse. Even though it was already half-melted, he could clearly make out black hair and white circle tattoos on her cheeks. This woman was not Siren. She was another dancer from the club.

"How is that possible?" Colin asked.

This woman must have been wearing Siren's clothes. Perhaps there was a mix up in the changing room. Or maybe they swapped bubbles on purpose.

He heard the sound of cop ball sirens coming down the street. Looking at the soggy corpse one more time to make sure it was really somebody else, he took off rolling across the alleyway, turning down a side street and disappearing into the shadows.

"I can't believe it," Colin said on the way home. "You're still alive, my love. I still have a chance."

But then a thought flashed through his mind. The news reports said none of the killings were done at random. The murderer was choosing specific dancers for execution. It was very possible that the killer was targeting Siren as his next victim, but got the woman wearing her clothing by mistake. That would mean Siren was still his next target. Tomorrow night, the killer would surely come back for her.

Right then and there, Colin vowed he would not let the same thing happen to the real Siren. He would stop the killer and protect his love. No matter what it took.

CHAPTER FOUR

Colin's account was charged a thousand dollars by the time he got back into his neighborhood, but it was not yet withdrawn. The amount was supposed to go toward rent and other bills. Although he wasn't on the police wanted list, breaking curfew meant he was just days away from being thrown out on the streets.

When he turned the corner onto his block, he saw the lights up ahead. A dozen cop balls were rolling onto the street as he arrived, their lights strobing within their blue plastic bubbles. Colin ducked behind a neighbor's hedge.

A cop ball with a metal encasing rolled up Colin's driveway and rammed open his front door. Then the cops flooded into his home through the round portal, shouting and aiming revolvers from tiny gloves that stuck out the sides of their bubbles.

"Damn," Colin said. "What do they want?"

He wasn't sure if he had broken the next hour of curfew or if he was somehow witnessed at the scene of the murder. There seemed to be a lot of them. It couldn't have been for something so small as breaking curfew.

Colin went back the way he came. His wrist computer was off, so they couldn't track him. But that also meant he couldn't use it for anything. He wouldn't be able to buy food or operate worker drones. He had no idea how he was going to protect Siren if he was wanted by the police.

Colin rammed through the door of a small white house a few blocks away, trying to get off the streets before the cop balls found him. When he closed the circular door and turned around, he saw a bubble staring at him. The image of a droopy female face stretched across its exterior.

"I'm sorry to disturb you," Colin said. "I didn't know anyone was home."

The woman kept staring at him. The sound of baby cries filled the room.

"You don't mind if I stay here, do you?"

She just stared.

"The fine for breaking the curfew is a thousand dollars an hour," he said to her. "I just don't have that kind of money and I live several hours away."

She just stared.

He wondered if there was even anyone inside of the bubble, until he moved into the living room and her head followed him.

"You won't call the police, will you?" he asked. "I'm really just trying to save some money."

Colin rolled past the plastic crib ball where the baby was crying. He couldn't see the baby inside. There was just a picture of a baby's head on the outside. It wasn't even a real baby picture—just a painting that likely came with the ball when it was purchased. Inside the ball, he could see the silhouette of the infant, sitting up with a pacifier in its hand, screaming to be held by its mother.

A worker drone was next to the crib ball, rocking it back and forth. But the drone seemed to be malfunctioning. It was an ancient machine and looked like a wicker man made of rusty barbed wire. Smoke poured from its neck and it rumbled loudly like a radiator that was about to explode. The child inside seemed terrified of it.

"Is he going to be okay?" Colin asked. The woman couldn't see him pointing at the infant. "I've heard they cry a lot, but I've never seen a real baby before."

The woman didn't answer his questions, continuing to stare at him. It seemed as if she had not left her home in years and had forgotten how to communicate with people.

Colin decided to explore her house.

"Mind if I have a look around?"

She just stared.

In the next room, a television was playing. It was inside a plastic containment room. There seemed to be somebody sitting on a bed watching it, but the room was too dark to tell for sure. All he could see was the glow of the television set behind the blurry plastic. The news was playing. A giant blond head was bobbing up and down on the screen.

"Police say they've uncovered the identity of the serial murderer known as *Kill Ball* late this evening," said the newscaster. "It is none other than star pool player Colin Hinchcliff. For those who don't remember, Colin was the state's pride and joy when the sport was at its height of popularity last decade. But six years ago he was forced into an early retirement when he suffered a severe mental breakdown before a championship match."

Colin turned and looked at the woman behind him. She was still watching him carefully. He wondered if she realized who he was. He wondered if she was going to call the cops.

"Hinchcliff is still at large and at the top of the most wanted list," continued the newscaster. "He is reported to be wearing an eightball design for clothing, which is the same uniform he wore as a pool player." A picture of an eightball came on the screen. "If you see anyone matching this description contact the authorities immediately. For more on this story, we bring you to Pete Long, our expert in the field." A picture of a brown-haired bubble-head came on the screen. "Pete, what can you tell us about Colin Hinchcliff, the notorious Kill Ball?"

"It makes perfect sense for somebody like Hinchcliff to be the person behind these horrible crimes," said Pete Long. "He has a history of violence. He accidentally killed his mother when he was a child. Then he killed his abusive father in self-defense as a teenager. With that kind of history, just about anybody would go over the edge."

"Wasn't he also responsible for the death of a teammate?" asked Linda.

"Yes, Rick Hudson who played cue ball," said Pete Long. "Hinchcliff was famous for being one of the most vicious players in the league and during one match he ruptured Hudson's containment field while trying to score a point. They were known to be close friends and Hinchcliff never quite recovered from that tragedy. He was institutionalized two months later, after attacking a fan outside of the pool arena. The doctors said he was having a schizophrenic episode and wasn't quite aware of what he was doing."

"Do you think Hinchcliff is aware of what he's doing while carrying out these executions?" Linda asked Pete Long.

"I'm certain he is," said Pete Long. "Unlike the unfortunate incident with the sports fan, these murders were well planned out in advance. Hinchcliff is a regular at all of the establishments where his victims were employed. He was even reported to have assaulted the latest victim, Shanya James, only minutes before her death."

"Let's hope he's brought into custody soon," said Linda, turning back to the camera. "Once again, if you have any knowledge on the whereabouts of Colin Hinchcliff, contact your local authorities immediately."

Colin had no idea that the police believed him to be the serial killer. What worried him most was that he wasn't even reported as a suspect. They reported that he was indeed the Kill Ball. And because the story broke so quickly, Colin believed it only meant one thing. The cops needed to close the case as soon as possible, whether they had the right man or not.

Colin stayed the night in the strange house, but the residents never said a word to him. In fact, the woman never even moved from her spot, just staring at Colin with her expressionless balloon-like face.

He had their worker drone make him breakfast, sterilize it, and attach the food compartment to the side of his bubble. Without being able to use money, he didn't know when he would get a chance to eat next.

When he finished eating, he filled a bag of stool and left it in the food compartment for the drone to dispose. The machine was so rickety that it seemed like it would fall apart on him at any minute.

Colin needed a disguise. He knew people would recognize his eightball uniform if he went anywhere in public. With all the cop balls patrolling the streets looking for him, he wouldn't last very long before getting caught.

"You don't happen to have a spare travel ball do you?" Colin asked the woman in the living room.

She stared at him.

"I have one at my place but I can't go there now," he said.

Colin searched through their home, but there didn't appear to be an extra anywhere.

He wondered what was wrong with the woman in the living room. She seemed to be mentally ill. Perhaps she was a deaf mute or too frightened of the intruder to say or do anything. Her infant cried within its crib ball all night. She did nothing to comfort it.

Outside, Colin found the only solution available to him. He was going to have to cover his clothing with mud. There was a vacant lot a few houses down where rockman-shaped worker drones were constructing a home. Colin rolled around in the dirt until his plastic bubble was covered. Darkness filled his ball as the coating blocked out the sun. He could only see through small patches where the mud didn't adhere.

"This will have to do," he said.

As he turned to leave, a giant head with a bushy black mustache rolled by on the side walk.

"Quit playing in the mud, ya dumbass," he said to Colin.

The mustache head was walking a poodle-terrier which yapped ferocious high-pitched hyper-yaps at Colin. As the man's plastic ball rolled, his dog's leash became shorter and shorter from being twisted up into knots, choking the dog's yaps into scratchy coughs.

People stared at him as he rolled into town, leaving a muddy trail down the rubber walkway. They assumed he was some kind of scummy hobo, but nobody suspected him to be the wanted killer.

Anyone who stared at Colin for too long, he would just say, "Can you spare some change?" in order to make his disguise appear more authentic.

And then they would divert their eyes and ignore him.

"Anyone?" he told a few school girls who were pointing at him and giggling. "Change?"

They sped away.

It was rare for people to encounter the homeless. Not many of them survive for long out on the streets. Without being able to afford upgrades for their plastic bubbles, it wouldn't take much for their seals to break. And without owning a personal worker drone, just being able to eat or dispose of waste was incredibly difficult.

"How can you stand being in there all the time?" a street

punk asked Colin as they walked together down the block.

The kid was not wearing clothes shaped like his face. He was wearing a big white ball with a red anarchy symbol painted on the front. The sound of violent punk rock was playing within his bubble, probably from headphones around his neck.

"I heard homeless people get insanely claustrophobic being stuck in their travel balls for months at a time," said the anarchy ball. "I don't think I could handle that."

Colin didn't want to engage him in conversation.

"I'd probably break the seal myself just to get one last breath of fresh air," he said.

"Don't remind me," Colin said, not sure he could keep up the act if the kid asked too many questions. Colin really didn't know much about what it was like to be homeless.

"Not to mention the smell," said the anarchy ball. "I heard you guys never get to take showers. You're just trapped in there with your own filth."

He needed to get rid of this kid.

"I said don't remind me," Colin said. "Get lost."

"Oh, sorry, man," said anarchy ball. "I'm just interested. I always wondered what it would be like to live on the streets."

"Leave me alone," Colin said, and sped up.

"Fine, asshole," said the anarchy ball. "I thought you could use the company." When Colin was far ahead of him, the punk yelled. "I probably would have given you a couple bucks if you weren't such a prick."

But Colin didn't look back.

After a few more blocks, Colin realized somebody was following him. It wasn't the anarchy ball. It was somebody inside of a giant Asian man's head. The Asian face had shiny black hair and dark sunglasses.

Colin turned a few corners, but the man kept following him. It wasn't hard to track Colin since he was still leaving a trail of mud everywhere he went. Colin had to act natural. He couldn't speed up or try to lose him. That would make him too suspicious.

The man quickly caught up to him, rolling right next to Colin's muddy bubble. Colin could sense him staring as they walked, looking through the sunglasses painted on the outside of his bubble.

"Can you spare some change?" Colin asked him, trying to act in the way a genuine homeless person might act in his situation. "My account is withdrawn. I haven't eaten in two days."

The Asian head didn't respond to the question. He appeared to be suspicious. It was as if he knew Colin was far too dirty, even for a homeless man.

Instead, he said, "Are you homeless?"

Colin cleared his throat. He tried to sound more beaten and hoarse. "Yes. Just a few dollars would help."

"Why aren't you at the station then?" he asked.

Colin had no idea what he was talking about.

"All vagrants were supposed to report to the police station earlier this week. They don't want you on the streets while the curfew is in effect."

"Ummm..." Colin tried to think fast.

"If you were out on the street last night without money in your account, you're probably on the wanted list. What's your name?"

"What?" Colin froze up.

"I'm a detective," said the Asian head. "If your name's on the wanted list you're going to have to come with me."

He rolled to his side and a hidden police badge lit up on the exterior of his bubble, glowing blue like a hologram.

"But..." Colin panicked. "I'm not *really* homeless."

"You said you were homeless."

"I am homeless, but—"

"You are or you aren't. Which is it?"

"I'm homeless, but I haven't been sleeping on the streets," Colin said. "I've been staying with a friend."

"Your friend lets you in his house with all that mud on you?" asked the detective.

Colin trembled inside his ball. He hoped it wasn't making his entire bubble shake.

"This just happened a couple of hours ago," Colin said. "I took a shortcut through a vacant lot and didn't realize how muddy it was until I was halfway through."

"You're supposed to stay on the walkway," said the detective. "When you go off-roading, you're bound to run over sharp rocks or stray pieces of metal. There's no law against it, but it's suicidal."

"I'm sorry," Colin said, trying to roll away from the cop. "I'll make sure not to do it again."

The detective rolled in front of him.

"Hold on," he said.

"Aren't we done here?" Colin asked.

"Almost," said the detective. "But you haven't given me your name yet."

"Oh," Colin said. "What for? I told you I'm staying with a friend."

"You asked for change, didn't you?" said the detective. "How am I going to transfer money to your account if you don't give me your name?"

Colin had to feign delight in the cop's offer, but nothing could have freaked him out more. He wanted to decline the cop's generosity, but that would have been far too suspicious. He had to give him a fake name. He had no idea what he was going to do.

"Pete James," Colin said. It was the first name that popped into his head. He prayed there was a Pete James out there.

He heard the detective typing on his computer inside his bubble.

"Pete James?" he said. "Hmmm…"

The detective was typing slowly. He didn't say anything for a few minutes. The silence drove Colin crazy. After a few more minutes, Colin thought the cop was holding him in suspense on purpose.

"Huh, there's no Pete James in my system," said the detective. "Weird. It must be some kind of error."

"An error?"

"Yeah, that happens sometimes," said the detective. "Is it Pete James or Peter James."

"Both," Colin said. "Either one."

Another long pause.

"Huh. Neither are coming up. Let me try James Peter."

Colin stared into his giant sunglasses as he typed.

"Nothing," said the detective. "Has your account been overdrawn for too long? If they put a hold on your account it wouldn't show up in my database."

"Yeah," Colin said, trying not to sound too excited about it. "That's probably it. I haven't been paying attention."

"Mooching off that friend of yours, no doubt," said the detective. He laughed a short firm laugh.

"Yeah," Colin said. "He's helped me out a lot."

"Well, sorry, buddy," said the detective. "I guess I can't help you out."

"It's no problem," Colin said. "Thanks anyway."

Colin inched away from him.

"Have a good day now," said the detective. "Take care of yourself."

"I will," Colin said.

When Colin turned and rolled down the sidewalk, he let out a long exhale, trying to calm his breathing. He rolled as fast as he could without looking suspicious.

"Wait a minute," yelled the giant Asian head. "Not so fast."

Colin stopped in his tracks.

The detective rolled toward him.

"You wouldn't be Peter *Hugh* James from Ling Beach would

you?" said the detective.

"Uh, yeah," Colin said.

He didn't turn around.

"How stupid of me," said the detective. "I was only searching within this district. You should have told me you're from across the river."

Colin began to tremble again, twice as much as before.

"Sorry, I wasn't thinking," Colin said.

"No problem," said the detective. "There. I just sent it."

"Thanks," Colin said.

"Did you get it?"

"Uh, not yet," Colin said.

He pretended to be operating his wrist computer, even though it was turned off.

"I want to make sure you get it," said the detective. "It would be a shame if I sent it to the wrong person by mistake."

Colin waited for as long as he thought it would take.

"There, it came through," he said. "Thanks a bunch."

"Thanks a bunch?" said the detective. "I just sent you fifty bucks and that's all you have to say? I thought you'd be a lot more excited about that."

"Oh, wow," Colin feigned excitement. "Sorry, I thought it was just five dollars. I didn't realize you sent fifty! You're a lifesaver. Thank you!"

"No problem," said the detective. "I know how tough it can be to be broke in this world of ours. I lost my brother to poverty."

"I'm sorry to hear that," Colin said.

"Don't worry, it was a long time ago," said the detective. "People die a lot these days."

"Thanks again," Colin said, turning to continue down the walkway.

The detective didn't move or say anything else. He just watched Colin from his spot, staring at him through his giant sunglasses.

CHAPTER FIVE

Depressing red-orange splashes of light bounced off of the rubber pavement as the sun set behind the cityscape. Wockobots chirped like electronic cicadas outside of restaurants and apartment buildings. Giant human heads rolled languidly through the summer warmth. Hippie balls rocked slowly back and forth in the dead brown grass of the park, clam-baking inside of their bubbles.

Colin managed to avoid capture all day, but with the night coming it was going to get far more difficult. He knew the real Kill Ball would come after Siren next. He had to protect her while avoiding capture. He had to warn her at the very least.

In line at Luscious Ladies that night, Colin hoped they weren't charging a cover. It was usually free to get in unless it was a busy night, like most weekends. Judging by the size of the line, it was possible he would be turned away. The rolling heads behind him kept their distance, somewhat disturbed by his grubby appearance.

"What's up with this guy?" he heard a voice say behind him.

"He's like Pigpen from those old cartoons," said another.

When he got to the front of the line, Colin recognized the bouncer at the door. It was Franko, the same bouncer who confronted him the night before.

"What the hell are you doing in my line?" Franko yelled, his face turning sour at the sight of Colin. "Get the hell out of here, bum ball."

Colin felt himself shrinking inside his bubble, but he knew he had to stand up to the guy. He had to get inside to keep an eye on Siren.

"You can't discriminate against me because of my appearance," Colin said.

Franko chuckled in that smug way only bouncers chuckle.

"I can turn away anyone I want," said Franko. "You think the girls want to get that shit all over them?"

"They don't have to touch me," he said. "I just want to watch."

"Wash yourself, get a job, and come back when you have some money," said Franko. "I don't want to see you here until then."

Colin rolled forward.

"But you have to let me in," he said.

The bouncer shoved him back. "I don't have to do anything. Now get out of here before I pop you."

As he bumped Colin again, a large section of dried mud crumbled from his ball, revealing the number eight. The bouncer recognized it immediately.

"You're him," Franko cried, rolling forward. "You're the son of a bitch who killed Shanya!"

The other bouncers heard him and rolled out of the door.

"It's Kill Ball!" Franko yelled.

The men in line rolled out of the way as Colin backed up.

"Somebody call the cops," another bouncer said.

Giant heads gathered all around them.

"I didn't kill her," Colin said. "You have to believe me."

Franko rolled forward, shoving customers out of the way.

"Fuck the cops," said Franko. "I'm killing this guy myself."

"Wait!" Colin cried.

As Franko charged him, Colin spun out of the way like a coin on its side. As a professional pool player, Colin was a master of dodging and striking within his ball.

"You're not getting away from me," Franko yelled.

Colin held up his hands within his bubble. "You don't understand…"

The bouncer charged again, trying to ram him against a wall, but Colin slipped past his face and orbited him like a moon around a planet.

"Come on," Colin cried. "I had nothing to do with the girl's death. I swear."

"I'll kill you," Franko yelled.

The bouncer shoved forward, trying to back Colin into a corner so that he would have nowhere to run. But Colin was really the one leading him into the corner. When Franko put all of his force into a charging ram, Colin used this force against him. He orbited to the left and sideways-slammed the bouncer's ball so hard that the large man flipped backward. He somersaulted within his bubble and landed head-first into the wall.

"Just let me go," Colin said. "I was a professional pool player. You're no match for me."

Franko stood up within his bubble. Even though Colin couldn't see him, he could tell he was dizzy and concussed inside of there. His ball rolled from side to side as he staggered forward.

"Take it easy," Colin said.

When the bouncer got into range, he used all his strength to punch Colin. But he used too much strength. His fist broke through his plastic bubble, missing Colin completely. The crowd of rolling heads screamed when they saw it.

"Sick bastard," Franko said, as his arm melted like taffy from the hole in his bubble.

Colin looked around. Everyone was watching. Even dancers were standing out there, naked in their bubbles. Siren didn't seem to be among them.

"He killed him," a woman cried.

"He really is the Kill Ball," said a man.

"First Shanya and now Franko," cried one of the dancers.

When Colin heard the sirens of cop balls rolling down the street, he charged at the crowd of bouncing heads. They gasped when they saw him coming at them and then spread apart to let him through.

When the cop balls arrived, the other bouncers pointed in the direction Colin ran. Three of the four cop balls followed after him.

The cop balls chased after Colin through the rubber streets. They couldn't see him up ahead, but they could follow the trail of dried mud he left behind. He could hear them gaining on him as he went through the streets, knocking over pedestrians and wocko-bots that got in his way.

"Sorry," Colin cried, as he sent an old lady ball spinning across the walkway, shrieking at the top of her lungs.

Then he slammed into a group of drunk college guys and they clacked against each other like marbles, spreading out across the walkway.

"Whoa, bro," one cried as he rolled backward, spilling his beer inside his bubble. "Look out."

When the cop balls came around the corner, they couldn't get through the crowd of rolling drunken frat balls. Colin was able to get ahead of them, turn corners, try to lose them. But there were more cop ball sirens up ahead. They were coming for him on all sides.

Then Colin turned down an alleyway and ran face to face with a giant head.

"Going this way?" said the giant head.

Colin recognized him. It was the Asian detective from earlier in the day. His blank face stared at Colin through oversized sunglasses.

"You?" Colin asked.

He backed away from the detective.

"You don't want to go that way do you, Colin Hinchliff?" said the detective. Colin could sense a smile appear on the man's face within his bubble. "If you go in that direction they'll catch you."

Colin didn't move, waiting for the detective to make a move.

But the detective did not show any sign of aggression. He did not draw a gun or tell him he was under arrest. Instead, the detective moved aside and allowed him to pass.

Colin did not hesitate. He rolled past the detective into the alleyway and hid inside the shadows.

When three of the cop balls arrived, the detective blocked their view of Colin. He told them that the assailant had continued down the street. The cop balls did not question him. Even though the mud trail ended at the alleyway, they sped off in the direction they were given.

"Get across the river," the detective said to Colin. "And run as far away from here as you can."

Colin rolled out of the shadows.

"Who are you?" Colin asked.

The detective was obviously smoking a cigarette inside of his bubble. Colin could see the red cinder glowing through one of the giant lenses of his sunglasses.

"My name is Mike Park," said the detective. "I'm in charge of the Kill Ball investigation."

"Why are you letting me go then?"

"I told you," he said. "I'm in charge of the Kill Ball investigation. You obviously are not Kill Ball."

Colin said, "How did you know?"

"I've seen him before," said Park. "You couldn't possibly be the same man I've encountered. Kill Ball's a murderer unlike anyone I've ever come across. He's not human. He's a soulless predator. A machine."

"He has to be stopped," Colin said.

Park said, "That's what I plan to do."

He rolled backward to the end of the alley.

"Forget about that dancer you've been obsessing over," said Park. "You're only going to get yourself killed. Or worse, you could get yourself caught. If they frame you for these murders Kill Ball might go into hiding for a while. I can't have that."

"I'm not going to let her die," said Colin.

48

Park's head bubble turned away.

"She doesn't even know you exist," said Park. "Forget about her and run."

"I can't..." Colin said.

But the detective already turned the corner. When Colin followed after him, he was nowhere in sight. The only sign that Park had ever been there was a cloud of English tobacco smoke that had seeped from his ventilation ducts.

Colin was grateful for the help, but he didn't care what the detective said. He had to save Siren. He knew Mike Park could care less if she survived the night. Guys like that only cared about meeting their goals. Anything that got in their way was just collateral damage.

It would still be a while before Siren got off of work, so Colin decided it would be best to find a place on her route home to watch out for her. He rolled up a ramp onto the roof of a quiet office building, where all windows were dark save one. A janitor ball was up there, listening to opera and reading comics.

On the roof, Colin had a good view of the street for six blocks in each direction. He would surely see Siren coming long before the Kill Ball could attack. The area between here and the club was far too populated for a murder to go unseen. No, Kill Ball would wait until she was at least this far away before striking.

But then Colin had a terrible thought. He didn't know if he would be able to recognize Siren. The other girl was wearing her bubble the night before and it was damaged beyond repair. What bubble would she be taking home?

He also wondered if this were even her route home. It could have been the route to Shanya's home. Perhaps the two women swapped bubbles every night and Colin had been following Shanya home all this time. There was also the chance that Siren didn't come into work that day. With the death of her close friend, she might have been too emotionally distressed to go back to work. Or she could be under police protection if they figured out she was Kill Ball's next target.

Colin didn't know what to do. He decided his only option was to stay there and wait. It was possible that Siren did go to work that day and would be walking home in Shanya's bubble. He would surely recognize Shanya's bubble. Since he saw her dead body, the image of her face had been burned into Colin's memory all night.

CHAPTER SIX

Screams echoed through the streets. A woman's screams. Colin jumped up from a sitting position so quickly he nearly rolled off of the roof.

"Yaaaaaa!" cried the woman's voice.

But he didn't see anything. He panicked. Was he too late? Was she already attacked?

There were a couple of pedestrians on the walkway who were also curious about the screams.

"No, no, no…" Colin said. "It can't be her."

She continued screaming. The screams were getting closer.

It was her. He recognized her tone of voice.

Then he saw her. She wasn't inside of Shanya's bubble. She was inside of her translucent bubble, the one she danced in. She was naked, flying down the block at top speed, screaming at the top of her lungs.

"Kill Ball," Colin said. "Where is he?"

He had to be behind her somewhere, chasing her. Colin had to stop him.

But when Siren reached the pedestrians on the walkway below, she didn't cry to them for help. Instead, she flashed them her tits and said, "Up yours, douchebags!" Then she continued flying down the street.

Siren wasn't being chased by the Kill Ball.

She was streaking.

Colin watched Siren as she rolled naked through the street. It was staggering to see an actual human being running down the road instead of a giant rolling head. If Colin squinted his eyes he only saw the woman and not the clear plastic barrier around her.

"Fuck all you uptight bitches!" Siren screamed.

She held the roof of her bubble so that she cartwheeled with the ball as she rolled, crying out with glee as if she were having the time of her life. Or maybe she was incredibly high.

Colin couldn't help but smile. Seeing her alive and full of energy made him so happy. Her bright purple peacock hair was so dazzling that it looked like a violet-colored flame inside a candle bowl.

In order to follow her, Colin had to jump from rooftop to rooftop. His bubble was a sports ball, the same kind he used when he was a professional pool player. Sports bubbles were a lot stronger than average travel balls and were a lot more flexible. Colin was able to bounce himself high into the air, leaping across alleyways, from building to building.

As he jumped, Colin watched Siren below. She was lubricated within her bubble, so she could swim inside of it just as she would onstage. As her ball rolled downhill, she dropped onto her belly and slid down the walkway like she was on a water slide. A fish swimming downstream.

"Woooooo!" she cried, giggling.

Then she got to her feet and went down the hill like a surfer, legs spread and arms out for balance, her ball rolling around her as she stayed in one place.

"Suck my balls, prudes!" she cried, though nobody was left on the streets to hear her but Colin.

Her screams of defiance were the most beautiful music Colin had ever heard. He couldn't believe such a passionate human being still existed in this world. He loved her even more than ever. She was an angel. A mermaid from heaven.

Colin was so enraptured by her wild attitude that he didn't notice the black leather bubble emerging from the shadows, following close behind.

Siren was so drunk on excitement that she didn't realize the road curving up ahead. She was cartwheeling within her bubble and not paying attention to where she was going.

"Look out," Colin whispered. He wanted to yell it out to her to warn her, but decided it would be better if he didn't give away his position.

She rolled straight into a storefront window and slammed into the glass, tumbling over herself. There was silence for a minute after impact, her limbs knotted around her body like a pretzel. Then she laughed out loud, lying upside-down inside of her bubble.

"Please be careful, my love," Colin whispered. "Your bubble is too thin and fragile to go banging into things haphazardly."

Siren continued laughing, rolling over, rubbing the blue spiral tattoos on her naked buttocks.

"Stupid store," Siren yelled, slamming into the glass with her ball. Then she giggled drunkenly.

The Kill Ball was closing in on her, using her collision as the perfect opportunity to attack.

"What the fuck, Shanya!" Siren screamed at the sky. "What am I going to do without you!"

She rolled backward into the middle of the street, staring up at the moon.

"Get your ass back here, you sexy bitch!" Siren hollered to the heavens. "Life won't be the same without you!"

Colin had no idea what she was doing. She appeared to be laughing and crying at the same time. She was beginning to seem like a crazy person.

Then he saw the black leather ball coming up behind her. The killer drew his knife, rolling slowly toward her back.

Colin had to act fast. First thing, he flipped a switch on his arm and powered up his wrist computer. The cops were after him, so they'd know where he was the second he turned on the device. Backup would be there soon, but they wouldn't get there in time to save Siren. That would be Colin's job.

"Look out," Colin yelled, but Siren was so delirious she didn't hear him.

Colin knew what he had to do. On the other side of the road, there was a ditch. He was going to have to bounce down from the rooftop and slam the Kill Ball off the side of the road. It would give Siren time to get away before the cops arrived.

But then Colin saw the blade pointed out of Kill Ball's side. If he jumped down at him he would end up landing on the blade, popping his bubble.

The Kill Ball froze as if preparing to charge knife-first.

Colin didn't have time to hesitate. He had to act.

As the leather ball charged forward, Colin leapt from the roof. But he didn't aim for Kill Ball, he aimed for Siren's bubble. On impact, the dancer shrieked as she went flying off the road into the ditch. She was only inches from the killer's knife and didn't even know it.

In the middle of the street, standing face to face with the man in the leather bubble, Colin wasn't sure what to do next. Kill Ball turned away from Siren to face Colin. The man in black was even more menacing this close. His bubble was perfectly spherical and it didn't wobble or shift as most bubbles did. Colin was usually able to read people, even though he couldn't see them inside their bubbles. But he didn't sense anything from Kill Ball. No emotion at all.

"Who the hell are you?" Colin asked him.

Kill Ball just stood there, facing him. The blade reflecting the street light in his eyes.

"Get your kicks from killing women?" Colin said, trying to distract him until the police arrived. "You can't fuck them so you have to stab them? Is that it?"

Colin noticed he was shaking in his bubble.

"Do you think of that knife as a dick?" Colin said.

The man in the black ball rolled toward Colin, but then froze when he heard the voice calling from behind.

"Who the fuck did that?" Siren yelled up at them from the ditch. The ledge was steep, so she couldn't see the road from down there. "What the hell just happened?"

Colin rolled to the side and yelled down at her, "Run. Get the hell out of here, now!"

She looked up at him, "What the hell's your problem?"

The Kill Ball turned away from Colin and rolled toward the ditch.

"He's trying to kill you," Colin yelled.

The Kill Ball rolled into the ditch before he could stop him, but as he went down Siren was coming up.

"You!" she shrieked, charging at Colin. "You're the asshole who killed Shanya!"

She rolled onto the road and slammed into him.

"You motherfucker," she yelled, slamming him again. Her face snarling, her tits slapping viciously against her bubble as she rammed him with all of her strength. "I'm going to fucking kill you!"

"I didn't kill her," Colin said.

"Then who did?" she cried.

She bounced her bubble into the air and drop-kicked Colin right in the face. Because her bubble was so thin and flexible, she was able to nail him with all her strength without breaking her bubble. He fell on his back.

"I'm here to help you," Colin said, getting to his feet while rubbing the blood from his broken lip.

She jump-kicked him again, this time in the chest. Colin was amazed by how acrobatic she was.

"Behind you," Colin said. "He's the one who killed your friend."

She turned but didn't see anyone. Kill Ball was still in the ditch.

"Don't fuck with me," Siren yelled. "There's nobody there. Everyone knows you're the eightball freak who killed Shanya. There were witnesses."

"I was at the scene of the crime," Colin said. "But I didn't kill her."

Colin looked through her bubble, over her shoulder, but Kill Ball wasn't there. What was he waiting for?

Police sirens roared through the streets.

"You can explain it to the cops, fucker," Siren said.

Then she head-butted him through the plastic and he fell back to the ground.

"How the hell are you so tough?" Colin cried, while rubbing his forehead.

The police were almost there, but Kill Ball was nowhere to be seen.

Police lights strobed through the sky, sirens roaring, as two cop balls flew down the road toward them. They pulled up behind Siren. Then two more cop balls came around the corner.

Colin was completely surrounded by the police and Siren had him pinned to the ground. Her knee was stretched out of her plastic and leaning against Colin's shoulder, shoving his face downward.

"This is him," Siren yelled. "He's the sicko who killed my Shanya!"

The men in the cop balls reached through tiny gloves on the sides of their bubbles and drew small handguns from holsters attached to the exterior.

"Get away from him," a cop said to Siren.

Though Siren was in the way, they still aimed their guns at Colin.

"Don't bother arresting him," Siren said. "Just kill the son of a bitch."

Colin wanted to cry. Even though he knew it was a misunderstanding, it hurt to hear his love say she wanted him dead.

"Step back ma'am," said the cop. "He's dangerous."

Siren stepped away from him and said, "He's such a disgusting pig."

With her out of the way, the cops came at him. Colin didn't move. He didn't want to get shot.

"It's not me," Colin told them. "I'm not the killer."

"Lie down on the ground," yelled the cops frantically. "Get down! Lie down!"

Their guns were getting shaky as they inched toward him. Colin could tell they were ready to fire at any second.

"Kill him already," Siren yelled, but the cops bumped her out of the way as if telling her to keep quiet.

"Cover yourself up, you filthy whore," one of the cops whispered to her in a venomous tone.

"The real killer is behind you," Colin said. "He went off the street into that ditch."

"Just shut up and get on the ground now," yelled a cop, moving forward.

Colin just saw him as a big blue ball with a badge on its front and a tiny hand holding a gun on its side. He decided it would be best to comply. Colin got down on the ground, lying on the bottom of his bubble. His legs curved upward behind him.

"Just look for yourself," Colin said. "He's there. He wants to kill her."

A cop spoke to his dispatcher, reporting that they had the suspect in custody.

"We're taking him in now," said the cop.

He pointed his gun back at Colin. The tiny hand sticking out of the bubble was barely able to aim.

"If you're not going to do it I'll do it myself," Siren told the cops.

She went for one of the cops' guns, trying to grab it through her plastic.

"Stand down," the cops yelled at Siren.

They turned their guns on her. "Let go of the weapon."

With their guns pointed at Siren, Colin stood up.

"Don't you dare hurt her," Colin yelled.

They turned their guns on Colin.

"Get back on the ground!" a cop yelled.

Siren still struggled to get the gun away from the cop.

"He deserves to die," she yelled.

She twisted her ball around, slamming into the cop. The gun slipped from his fingers but she couldn't get a good grip on it herself through the plastic. The weapon thumped against the rubber street.

"That's enough foolishness," said another cop ball, knocking her away from the weapon.

The police man retrieved the weapon on the ground with his tiny gloved hand and handed it back to his partner.

"We're taking both of you in as soon as the wagon gets here," he said.

Colin was the first to see it, over the police man's shoulder. The black leather ball stood silently in the center of the street.

"What the hell is that?" said a cop.

They all turned to the black bubble. The expression on Siren's face changed. She now knew Colin was telling the truth.

"That's him," Colin said. "That's the real Kill Ball!"

The cops didn't believe him.

"Get out of here," the cop told the black leather ball. "This is police business."

The man in the black ball did not move.

"I said get out of here," said the cop.

The ball turned, revealing a blade.

"He's got a knife," another cop cried.

They aimed their weapons at him.

"Put it down," said a cop.

The black ball did not move, holding the knife at them.

"I told you," Colin said. "He's the one you're after."

"Shut up," a cop said, going back and forth between aiming his weapon at Colin and the new assailant.

The cops surrounded the black ball.

"Something's not right about him," said Siren. "Don't get too close."

But the cops hushed her up.

"This is your final warning," said the lead cop. "Put the knife down now or—"

The cop's bubble exploded.

Nobody knew how it happened. They just suddenly saw his exterior explode into bits and then there was a naked middle-aged man standing there in the street. He was dead before he could even melt.

"Drop him," yelled another cop.

They fired at the Kill Ball, putting bullet after bullet into the bastard. The man in the black ball did not move. He let them shoot him over and over again. The bullets seemed to have no effect. His bubble did not pop.

Once the firing had stopped, Colin realized what killed the gray-haired cop. As the man's flesh melted to the ground, he saw a long pole of metal inside of the cop's chest cavity. The killer's knife was extendable.

Kill Ball took his time retracting his blade to normal size, as if unconcerned about the bullets being fired at him. The blade made a ticking noise with every inch it retracted.

"How is he still standing?" a cop asked.

"I landed every shot," said another. "He should be dead."

When the knife was back to normal size, the man in the black bubble faced the other policemen.

"Get away from him," Siren said, backing up. "His bubble has got some kind of bulletproof shielding. You can't hit him."

But the cops fired anyway.

During the time it took for Colin to blink, the Kill Ball took out all three of the cops. It lunged at them in a circular motion, cutting two of them down and ramming the third into the brick wall next to Colin.

Colin saw the damage. The two standing cops crumbled over as their flesh melted from their bones. The third cop was nowhere to be seen. The Kill Ball had rammed him so hard that his bubble popped and his body smashed through the brick wall. He was nothing but blood and liquid meat stuck to the front of Kill Ball's bulletproof exterior like a bug on a windshield.

"Run," Colin said.

He got to his feet and rolled away from the Kill Ball.

Siren was just standing there. It was as if she didn't realize all the cops were dead, that it was just the two of them left.

"We have to get out of here," Colin said.

The Kill Ball was stuck inside of the crumbled wall. Colin had no idea how any bubble could be strong enough to break through brick like that.

She broke out of her state of shock when Colin bumped his bubble into hers.

"You believe I'm not the killer now, right?" Colin asked. "Trust me then. I'm here to help you."

She looked at Kill Ball as he struggled to free himself, then back at Colin.

"Let's go," Colin yelled.

Then they rolled off, down the street, trying to get as far away from the Kill Ball as they could.

CHAPTER SEVEN

"Who the hell was that guy?" Siren cried. "How did he do all of that?"

They rolled at top speed, trying to get as far away as they could get.

"I have no idea," Colin said.

"Where do we go? What are we going to do?"

"More cops should be coming any minute," Colin said. "They think I'm the killer, so they're tracking me."

"That guy just tore through four cops," said Siren. "What good are they going to be?"

As he rolled at top speed, Colin scanned behind him for signs of police lights. There was no sign of more cops.

"When they find out what happened to the last group, they'll send a lot more than four men," Colin said. "They might even send in the SWAT balls."

"Call them then," Siren said, turning a corner. "Tell them they'll need armor-piercing bullets."

When Colin looked down at his wrist computer, he noticed the lights were out.

"Shit," Colin said.

He didn't remember turning it off. When trying to turn it back on, nothing happened.

"My phone's dead," Colin said.

"What?" Siren said.

"My computer isn't working at all," he said. "The cops aren't tracking us."

Siren looked down at her wrist.

"Mine too," she said. "What the hell's going on?"

Colin examined his computer.

"Kill Ball," Colin said. "He must have some device that fries our electronics. The same thing happened when he killed your friend Shanya last night."

The abrupt silence told Colin he shouldn't have mentioned her friend's name.

"What do we do now?" Her voice choked up as she spoke, the thought of her dear friend being killed by that maniac filled her mind with horrifying visions.

"We need to find someone with a phone and call the police station," Colin said. "There's a detective who I think will help us. If only we can get a hold of him."

The road sloped downhill and both Siren and Colin jumped on their stomachs, sliding down like frantic surfers.

There was no sign of Kill Ball as they entered an apartment building a few streets away. Although most buildings in that area were empty commercial properties, this was one that was obviously occupied by people. Most of the lights in the windows were on, glowing softly across the desolate street. Somebody had to be there who could help.

Colin slammed the door shut behind them. The electronic lock wasn't enough to stop Colin from breaking in, so it wouldn't hold the killer either. They had to hope he didn't see them enter.

"Do you think he's really coming after us?" Siren asked.

"I don't know," Colin said. "If there are too many cops out I'd imagine he'd give up and go into hiding. But to be on the safe side, we should assume he's still hunting you."

Siren was in agreement. She nodded in a twitchy, squirrelly way.

The lobby was wide and empty. A security station was to the right but there was no security guard behind the desk.

"You might want to cover yourself," Colin said to Siren as she wiped sweat from her naked breasts.

"Huh? Why?" Her voice was an annoyed tone.

"We need to ask these people for help," he said. "Your nudity might offend them."

She leaned her hand onto her hip, not covering herself in the slightest. "I don't give a shit. They'll help me or I'll knock them on their asses."

"You can't threaten them."

"Fuck the prudes," Siren said. "My life is on the line here."

They rolled up the ramp onto the next floor. The place was quiet. Not even the sound of televisions could be heard.

The first door they came to, Colin rolled into the doorbell three times. Then they waited.

"I can't do the talking," Colin said. "They've probably seen me on the news. They'll think I'm dangerous."

Siren switched places with him. He kept his distance. She didn't bother covering herself with her hands.

They continued waiting. Nobody came to the door.

"Let's try the next one," Colin said.

The occupants of the next apartment didn't open their door either. Nor did the ones in the next.

"Where is everybody?" she asked.

There was a large head rolling down the hallway toward them.

"Ah, there's someone," Siren said.

The exterior of the person's bubble was designed to look like a smiling double-chinned man with curly brown hair and bushy eyebrows.

"Hey, we need help," Siren said to him.

They went toward the man.

"Can you call the police for us?" she asked him. "It's an emergency."

The man didn't react to her. He kept rolling down the hallway. He rolled right past them and continued on his way.

"What's up with that guy?" Siren asked.

She followed after him.

"Didn't you hear me?" she said. "We need help."

The man continued rolling. It was almost as if nobody was inside of there, like it was rolling on its own.

"Fuck this," Siren said. "I'm breaking one of these doors down."

She rammed into the next apartment, smashing through the door.

"What are you doing?" Colin said.

"We don't have time to be dicking around," she said, as she rolled into the apartment.

Inside, there was a family of four. Mother and father balls were in the center of the room. They turned their giant faces toward the intruders. The two children balls rolled around their parents. All four of them were silent.

"We need help," Siren said. "Can you phone the police for us?"

"Sorry about your door," Colin said. "But this is a matter of life and death."

The family balls just stared at him.

"What's going on here?" Siren said. "Why are they acting so weird?"

Colin had no idea. It was just like the house he had broken into the night before. There were clearly people inside the bubbles, but they seemed catatonic, in a daze.

"What the hell's your problem?" Siren yelled.

She charged at the father ball and slammed into him. He toppled backward, bouncing off the wall, and rolled across the floor like a lazy pool ball. Though his face was upside-down, he didn't bother correcting his position.

"Forget about them," Colin said. "There's got to be another way to call the cops."

Siren just shook her head slowly as she watched the father's bubble rock back and forth, upside-down, wondering what the man was doing inside of there that made him so quiet.

They went to the next apartment and broke open the door. The window was wide open. A strong wind blew through the curtains. There was only one resident here, but there was not much left of her. Colin could only tell it was a *her* because the remains of the broken bubble looked like a female face.

"Did she commit suicide?" Siren asked.

Beneath the deflated plastic was a pool of liquid meat.

"Possibly," Colin said, closing the living room window. "It could have been an accident."

"You don't think *he* did it do you?" she asked. "The murderer?"

Colin shook his head inside his bubble.

"The puddle has a thick film on it," Colin said. "She's been dead a few days at least."

"And nobody did anything about it?" she asked.

"Maybe she didn't have any friends," he said. "Nobody had a reason to check up on her."

Siren kneeled down within her bubble, staring at the puddle of flesh. "It's so sad."

Colin nodded. "Let's look around."

"Do you want me to sing you a lullaby?" asked a voice from the kitchen.

When they turned the corner, they saw a cartoon face staring up at them from the center of the room. It was a bright pink spider-shaped drone. A wocko-bot.

"Do you want me to sing you a lullaby?" repeated the wocko-bot. Its painted-on smile didn't move when it spoke.

Its electronic voice even higher pitched than other wocko-bots. A red bow was attached to the side of its pink-ball head.

"A wocko-bot?" Siren asked.

Colin didn't want to have to deal with a stupid wocko.

"Let's go," he said, turning to leave.

"Wait," said Siren. "It can help."

"How?"

"It's a wocko," she said. "They can call emergency hotlines."

Colin had no idea this model could do that.

"Wocko, call the police," Siren said.

The wocko tilted its smiling face at Siren.

"Okay," said the wocko.

It paused for an unnecessarily long period of time.

Then it asked, "Which branch of the police do you want?"

"I don't know," Siren said. "The closest one."

The wocko-bot paused, searching its database.

"Okay, I'll call," said the wocko.

Its sluggishness was driving Colin mad.

After a few minutes, the wocko said, "There is no one answering at that number. Shall I try another?"

"Call the cops," Colin said. "Any cops."

"Okay, I'll call," said the wocko.

A few minutes passed and the wocko said, "There is no one answering at that number. Shall I try another?"

"It's useless," Colin said. "I hate wocko-bots."

"Want to fight?" asked the wocko-bot.

"What?" Colin said.

"Want to fight?" it repeated. "Maybe wocko-bots hate you, too."

It didn't move from its spot, just staring up at them with a big smile on its face.

"Sorry," Colin said.

"Let's forget about the cops," Siren said. "If we just stay quiet in here we'll be fine."

"But if he knows we're here we'll be trapped," Colin said. "We'll have nowhere to escape. No, we have to speak to Michael Park."

Siren nodded at him.

"Okay, I'll call," said the wocko.

They stared at the pink spider robot as it placed another call, wondering what the heck it was doing.

After a few minutes, the wocko said, "I have a Detective Michael Park on the line. Would you like to speak with him?"

"Yes!" Siren yelled. "Put him through."

They heard him sighing on the other line before they heard him speak. The sound was coming out of the wocko-bot's face, as if the pink robot was the one sighing.

The first thing Detective Park said on the line was, "I thought I told you to forget about the dancer and get out of town, Colin."

"How'd you know it was me?" Colin asked.

"I had a hunch," said the detective, his voice was so calm he almost sounded bored. "Is the girl still alive?"

"Yes," Siren said.

"Good," he said. "Keep her alive. She's the only one who can clear your name. I'm tracing your location now."

There was a long pause.

"I want you to stay where you are," said Detective Park. "I'm coming to get you. Hold tight."

"Wait," Colin said. "You have to know that normal bullets won't work on the real Kill Ball. He's got some kind of armor. The other policemen couldn't touch him."

"I'm well aware of his capabilities," said the detective. "I'll be ready for him if he shows."

"Detective Park?" Colin asked.

"Yes?"

"He tore through four policemen like nothing," Colin said. "Who exactly is this guy? How could he do that?"

There was a pause.

"I'll tell you this," said Park. "He's not a psychopath who kills women for kicks."

"Then who is he?" Siren asked. "Why is he after me?"

Another pause.

"There are people out there who hate everything that you

stand for," he told her. "He is their weapon sent to eliminate you and everyone like you. And he won't stop until he finishes the job."

Siren didn't respond. She stared at the wall behind the spider drone, a little unnerved by the detective's words.

"What do you mean?" Colin said. "Who sent him?"

"I'll be there as soon as I can," said the detective. "Lie low until I get there."

When the cop was off the line, Colin and Siren looked at each other.

"Now what?" Siren asked.

"We wait," Colin said.

They were sitting in a back room away from the dead woman. The lights were off so it appeared as if nobody was home. Colin rocked back and forth within his ball, having a hard time holding still.

"What do you think he meant by the people who sent the Kill Ball?"

Siren didn't answer him right away.

"There's only one group he could possibly mean," she said, her bright blue eyes practically glowing in the dark.

"Who?"

"The Censorship Bureau," she said. "They're the ones who ruined our lives all those years ago. And they continue to ruin our lives in new ways each and every day."

"What do you mean?"

"You mean you've never heard the story?" Siren asked.

Colin hadn't a clue.

"They say the Censorship Bureau created the virus that put the human race inside of plastic bubbles," she said. "They synthesized it and purposely spread it across the globe. At least, those are the rumors."

"Why on Earth would they do that?"

"For the most ridiculous reason you've heard," Siren said. "To stop people from having sex."

She giggled as she heard herself say those words out loud.

"Supposedly, they were a group of moral crusaders who started a war against pornography," she said. "But they didn't stop with porn. They wanted to abolish sex altogether. They didn't even want people having sex for procreation, trying to replace natural breeding with in vitro fertilization. So they created the virus that forced people into separate bubbles. A virus that made it so nobody would ever touch anybody ever again."

"How do you know all of this?"

"It's just a rumor," she said. "It seems too ridiculous to be true, doesn't it? Why would anybody be so against sex that they'd go to such an extreme?"

"Do you believe it?" he asked.

"I don't know," she said. "I always thought of it more as a horror story that women in my profession told each other. We like to see ourselves as revolutionaries against the prudes. And the Censorship Bureau is our greatest enemy, out to put an end to us. But with so many of my friends dying, I'm beginning to wonder if there might be some truth to those stories about the Bureau."

"So they sent Kill Ball to end your profession?" Colin asked. "They want to get rid of all erotic dancers?"

"No," she said. "If the myths about the organization are true then there's an even stronger reason why they'd want me dead."

"What is that?"

"All the girls targeted by the Kill Ball, including myself, have discovered something that would send the Censorship Bureau into a fit of insane rage."

"What?"

A bright smile crossed her face.

"We've discovered a new way to have sex," she said.

CHAPTER EIGHT

Colin wasn't sure exactly what she was talking about. A new way to have sex? Without touching each other, sex was impossible. Nobody had had real sex with another human being in over two decades.

"I used to do it with Shanya," said Siren. "We had been lovers for months before she was murdered." She paused for a moment. "She was so fucking hot. It's such a fucking waste…"

She just looked down at her knees and shook her head.

"But how?" Colin said. "How did you do it?"

"Not just anyone can do it," Siren said. "Just some people. A small group of very special people."

She looked at him with her penetrating blue eyes, staring at him through his bubble.

"You see, I'm not exactly human anymore," she said. "I'm a new species. A mutant."

Colin thought she was fucking with him for a moment. But her face was completely serious.

"A mutant?" he asked. "What do you mean?"

"I've evolved," she said. "You think putting ourselves inside of plastic bubbles wouldn't have any effect on us as a species? Our bodies crave each other. Plastic isn't going to keep us apart. We've evolved to get beyond that barrier in order to have sex."

"But evolution doesn't happen so quickly," Colin said. "Maybe our children's children would start evolving in small unusual ways, but within our lifetime?"

Siren giggled at him.

"What?" he asked, wondering why she was laughing.

She shook her head. "In extreme conditions, it can happen.

Our evolution happened practically overnight. I believe it's because of our profession. We are so focused on sexuality night after night that our DNA took a leap forward. We became the first of a new species."

"But what exactly makes you a new species?" Colin said. "I don't get it."

Siren giggled at him again.

"What's so funny?" he asked.

She laughed louder.

"You're funny," she said. "You don't see it at all, do you?"

"See what?"

"My eyes," she said. "Don't they look unusual to you?"

"Yes," he said. "They're the most beautiful things I've ever seen."

He blushed when he realized what he was saying.

"Don't they look familiar?" she said.

"I've never seen anyone with eyes like yours before," he said. "They seem to glow in the dark. They are why I fell in love with you."

She laughed wildly at him. He realized he probably shouldn't have said that he was in love with her.

"Are you blind or what?" she said. "They should look very familiar to you."

"Why?"

"Because *you* have the same eyes," she said.

"What do you mean?" Colin said, rolling toward a mirror in the corner.

"It's not just dancers who have been evolving," she said. "Recently, some of our regulars have been following our lead. The men who are the most obsessed, the creepiest and most desperate, who come back night after night—those are the ones who have been evolving with us."

Colin looked at himself in the mirror.

"Men like you," she said.

Although the room was dark, even though he was inside of a black bubble, Colin could see them. It was faint, but he could definitely make out what looked to be two glowing eyes inside of his ball.

"You're becoming a male of our species," she said.

Then she laughed.

Colin continued staring at himself. He didn't feel any different. He didn't feel like he was becoming a new species. But it was unmistakable. Those were his eyes glowing back at him in the mirror.

"I'm surprised you don't remember," she told him. "When you were at the club last night, while I was giving you a lap dance, I experimented with you."

Colin turned away from the mirror to look at her.

"Didn't you feel yourself leave your bubble?" she asked. "We were embracing for at least a minute."

"You mean…"

Colin did remember the experience. His eyes were closed, but he felt himself being pulled inside of Siren's bubble with her. He thought it was a delusion caused by the sexual adrenalin. It was usually that way when he was given a lap dance.

"I had never been with a male before," she said. "When I realized you were one of us, I wanted to see what it was like."

"We had sex?"

She laughed. "No, we didn't go all the way. Not by a long shot."

Colin rolled across the room, pacing.

"I don't get it," he said. "How does it work? How did I leave my bubble?"

She waved him over.

"Come here," she said. "I'll show you."

Colin rolled up to her.

"Sit down," she said, placing her palms on the insides of

her ball. "Put your hands up."

Colin sat cross-legged and touched his hands to hers, feeling her through the plastic.

"Now relax," she said. "Push with your hands, but focus on my eyes. I'll pull you out."

"I don't know if I'm ready," Colin said.

"Don't you want to leave your bubble?" she said.

"I don't know."

"You must want to, deep down," she said. "Otherwise you wouldn't have evolved. Our species transformed into what we are because we were sick of being trapped in these tiny prisons. We had to break free."

Colin took a deep breath.

"Now look into my eyes," she said.

Colin looked into them.

Before he knew it, he felt their palms touching through the plastic. There was a glowing light inside of their hands. Then her fingers folded around his fingers.

Colin didn't break eye contact, but he began to tremble with shock. He was holding her hands through the plastic. He was really touching her.

"Ready?" she asked.

Before Colin could respond, she pulled back. He felt his arms leave his bubble. He gasped as if he were jumping into freezing water. She pulled him as far as she could, then she grabbed him by the elbow and pulled him more. He felt naked, really naked, for the first time since he was a child.

Once his face reached the edge of his bubble, he began to panic.

"Wait," he cried, turning his head.

She paused for a second. Then she smirked at him and pulled him the rest of the way in.

Colin felt himself spill inside of Siren's bubble, falling onto her body, touching her naked flesh. Her real naked flesh.

His face was inches from her face, looking deep into her blue eyes.

"Why, hello," she said to him, continuing to reel his lower half into the bubble. "It's nice to see the real you."

That's when Colin saw his own arms. They were no longer human.

"What's going on?" Colin said, looking at his hands.

His flesh was glowing bright blue.

"It's the new you," she told him.

Blue light radiated from her flesh.

"You see," she said, a glowing blue arm emerged from her human arm. "The way we escape our bubbles is to escape our own skin."

A shining blue figure pulled itself out of Siren's body like a spirit escaping a corpse. Her flesh fell limp. The light went out of her eyes. It was just a dead husk.

"This is the species we've evolved into," said the shining blue figure.

She smiled at him. Colin looked down at his body. He was the same as she was. They weren't human anymore.

Colin felt her arms wrap around him, rubbing her fingers against his glowing skin.

"I'm addicted to the feeling," she said. "Just touching each other's new flesh gives me a sense of euphoria."

She let him touch her. No, she urged him to touch her. When his fingers slid across her body, he knew exactly what she meant. It wasn't the same as human flesh. Touching her was like nothing he had ever felt before. It was like being able to physically hold an emotion in your hand.

"It's amazing," he said.

He didn't know what else to say. He felt himself crying. But his new body did not produce tears; it only created a tingling sensation around his cheeks.

"These are our inner bodies," she said. "It is everything we have inside us made flesh."

He curled his hand around her neck, felt the smooth top of her head where her hair had been.

"You feel like a thirst that has finally been quenched," he said.

"You feel like a child who has finally been let out to play," she said to him.

When Colin looked back at her empty flesh lying in the bubble beside them, he realized that he didn't find it beautiful anymore. What he saw inside her eyes was what he was really attracted to. Her inner body was what he loved.

As she kissed him, it felt like their bodies were merging together. Their energy flowed in and out of each other's mouths.

"What?" she said, pushing away from him. "Your skin?"

Colin looked. The light emanating from his inner flesh was turning purple. Then Siren's skin changed color.

"This has never happened before," she said. "Not with any of the women."

Then Colin noticed he had an erection. Although it didn't look quite the same as his human penis, it grew out from his thighs like a smooth beam of light.

"It's opening," Siren cried.

She was looking at her crotch. Her vagina separated, widening outward. Dark purple light glowed within. Then she saw Colin's penis.

"It's because you're a man," she said. "Our bodies are preparing themselves to mate."

They looked at each other for a moment. Then the next thing Colin knew she was wrapped around him, pulling him deep inside of her. They rolled themselves together and became a ball of glowing purple light, emanating from within the clear plastic bubble.

Back inside of their old bodies, in separate bubbles, they leaned against each other's backs.

"I want to stay in that form forever," Colin said.

"You can't," she said. "Most of your inner self can escape, but not all of it."

"Is that why my feet stayed inside my bubble?"

"Yeah," she said. "Your old body won't let you go. It always holds on to part of it. We can leave our bodies in order to mate, but we still need our old bodies in order to survive."

"So did we really just *mate*?" Colin asked.

"I don't know," she said. "I've never been with a male before. Until just days ago, there weren't any males. I don't know if that really counts as mating."

"But I thought you said mating was the whole reason why we evolved."

"Maybe," she said.

"If you're pregnant what will the baby be like?" Colin asked.

She did not seem to like that he brought up pregnancy at that moment. But then she thought about it for a minute. A smile grew across her face.

"Maybe it will be born without a human body," she said. "It would be so amazing if I had a child made entirely of its beautiful inner form."

Colin's smile grew twice as wide as Siren's. "Then he will never have to know what it's like to grow up inside of a plastic bubble."

"He'll be free to live as humans were meant to live," she said.

Then the smile fell from Colin's face.

"And he'll be able to hug his mother whenever he wants," Colin said. "Without accidentally killing her."

As tears hit his cheek, he felt as if the tear was the real him. And the cheek he was rolling down was just a big chunk of cold dead flesh.

When Siren noticed he was crying, she rubbed his shoulder through the plastic.

"I'm happy you weren't really the killer," she told him, feeling a little guilty about the way she tried to kill him earlier. "This world might have turned you into an awkward lonely creep, but now you're one of us."

Colin looked back at her and wiped his eyes.

"The new you isn't going to mold," she said. "It's going to shine."

"What's taking your detective friend so long?" Siren asked him. "Shouldn't he have been here by now?"

Colin rolled toward the window.

"Probably," he said.

There was nothing outside. The street was quiet, empty. All he could see was the dim street light shining against the rubber walkway.

"Let's try calling him back," Colin said.

In the kitchen, the wocko-bot turned to them and bounced up and down.

When it finished hopping, it said, "Would you like a pizza party?"

"No," Colin said.

He looked back at the open window, worried that the wocko's obnoxious voice would carry outside. The curtains were blowing in the breeze.

"Didn't you close the window?" Siren said.

Colin nodded. He swore that he had closed it before. He wondered if it blew itself open again.

"Call Detective Michael Park," Colin said to the drone.

"Okay, I'll call," said the pink wocko.

After a few minutes, the wocko said, "There is no one answering at that number. Shall I try another?"

"He's not there?" she asked.

They waited ten minutes and then tried calling him again. No one was picking up.

"I'm going to go outside and look around," Colin said. "Stay here."

"Don't," she said, rolling toward him.

"The detective could already be here," Colin said. "He might just not be able to find us."

"I'd rather we stuck together," she said.

"Would you like me to dance?" asked the pink robot, wobbling back and forth on its spindly metal legs.

"I'd rather you stay hidden," Colin told Siren, ignoring the drone. "You're the one he's targeting, not me."

"Would you like me to dance?" asked the wocko-bot.

"But if he's targeting evolved humans he'll come after you as well," she said.

"Would you like me to dance?" asked the wocko-bot.

"Not necessarily," Colin said. "I'll only be a few minutes."

"Would you like me to dance?"

"Let's just wait a while longer."

"Would you like me to dance?"

"I'll be right back. Don't move."

"Would you like me to dance?"

Colin rolled to the door and looked back at her.

"Hurry up then," she said.

Colin agreed.

"Would you like me to dance?"

After he was gone, Siren looked down at the pink robot smiling up at her.

"Would you like me to commit mass genocide?" asked the wocko-bot.

"What?" Siren cried.

"I mean..." the wocko-bot shook its head. "Do you want a pancake?"

Siren groaned and rolled out of the kitchen, trying to ignore the melted body lying on the living room floor. She didn't notice, but something was staring at her through the open window. A black leather ball was on the rubber walkway below, staring up into the room. The dim street lights glittered against the blade of a jagged metal knife.

CHAPTER NINE

Colin left the apartment. The hallway was empty.

On the ramp toward the upper floor, there was a window where he could view the street. There was nothing out there. No cop balls, no Detective Park, nobody at all.

Rolling down the hallway, he noticed many of the apartment doors had been smashed open. At first, he wondered if the Kill Ball had come looking for them. But then he noticed all the doors had been smashed open from the inside.

"Hello?" Colin asked one open apartment.

The lights were out. He decided not to enter.

In the next apartment, he called out, "Is everything alright in there?"

There was no answer. He rolled inside and looked around. Nobody was home. There weren't any people in any of the apartments on that floor.

"Where did they go?" Colin asked.

He went downstairs to the lobby. It was also empty. The front door of the apartment building was open.

Slowly rolling down the ramp, he peeked around the corner, making sure nobody was going to jump out at him. He hoped the police had arrived and ordered them all to evacuate the building. He hoped Kill Ball wasn't inside, roaming the hallways.

Colin pushed the front door closed. As the door shut, he heard a gunshot outside. He rolled backward. Two more gun shots. Then silence. They sounded distant. He wasn't exactly sure if they were really bullets.

He went back upstairs to return to Siren.

"Was there anyone out there?" Siren asked, as he closed the apartment door behind him.

"Nobody," Colin said. "There wasn't anyone in the building at all. Everyone disappeared."

"What do you mean?" she asked.

"Some doors have been smashed apart upstairs," he said. "Everyone's gone. It's like they ran away in a hurry."

"What about the family we saw earlier?" she asked. "The ones who wouldn't speak?"

"They're gone as well," Colin said. "Vanished without a trace."

"But why?"

"I don't know," Colin said. "But I don't like it. I don't think we should stay here any longer."

Siren didn't know what to say. She looked away from him, trying to think. She didn't like the idea of leaving, but she wasn't comfortable with staying either.

"I'll try the detective one more time," Colin said. "If we can't get a hold of him we'll leave."

Siren exhaled loudly. She wasn't very optimistic.

They tried the detective one more time. He didn't answer, but Siren didn't want to give up and leave just yet. They tried again. And when that didn't work, they tried to get a hold of somebody, anybody who could help them. They couldn't get through to anyone.

"What's going on?" Siren cried.

Colin shook his head.

"It's probably this piece of junk." Colin kicked the wockobot through his bubble. "It can't get through to anyone."

The drone fell over, whirring with anger.

"Or Kill Ball knows we're here," said Siren. "He was able to jam our electronics. Maybe he's able to stop our messages from getting out."

"In which case, he's probably just waiting for us to leave so that he can strike," Colin said.

"So should we stay?" she asked.

"No, we should go," he said.

The wocko-bot pulled itself to its feet and shook its head. Colin kicked it again, just to vent his frustration.

"Colin, are you there?" asked the wocko-bot.

It wasn't the robot speaking. Somebody was communicating through the drone. It sounded almost like Detective Park's voice.

"Park?" Colin asked. "Is that you?"

"Yes, it's me," Park said.

His voice was slow and warped, like a broken record. Siren rolled into the kitchen to hear more clearly.

"Are you okay?" Colin asked.

There was a long pause.

"Yes," said the detective.

Another long pause.

"Where are you?" Colin asked. "I thought you were coming to get us."

He could hear dripping noises coming from the other line, like a bathroom sink had been left on.

"There were complications," said the detective. "I sent a SWAT team to your area as well as several local officers."

A long pause.

"And?" Siren yelled. "What happened?"

A long pause.

"There were complications," said the detective.

His voice seemed to be slowing down, becoming even more warped.

"What complications?" Siren repeated. "Why aren't they here?"

A long pause.

"Change of plans," said the detective. "You have to come here, to the police station."

"Where is it?" Colin asked.

"The police station," he said. "Hurry." His voice was becoming muffled and unintelligible. "You... safe... soon..."

"Hello?" Colin asked. "We can't understand you."

The detective continued, "...on your own... only way..."

"Hello?" Colin said.

There was nothing else said on the other end. Just static. Colin couldn't tell if the detective had hung up or if he just stopped talking. The sound of dripping could still be heard on the other end.

"Come on," Colin said. "We have to move."

"Are we really going to the police station?" Siren said. "There was something severely wrong with that call. Did you hear his voice?"

"I'm sure it was just the wocko distorting the call," Colin said. "It's been buggy."

The pink wocko looked up at Colin and cocked its head, as if it had no idea what he meant by *buggy*.

"But that guy didn't sound anything like the detective we spoke to earlier," Siren said. "His voice was all warped. How do you know it was even him?"

"Who else would it be?"

"Who do you think?" Siren said. "He called us, remember? And then disguised his voice. He's just trying to get us out of the building."

"I don't know," Colin said. "If he knew we were here he could have just come in and killed us. We wouldn't be able to run away while trapped in here."

"I think he likes games," Siren said. "Killing us in here would be too easy for him."

"Or he could be long gone," Colin said. "Let's just go. I'd feel safer at the police station than in this place."

Siren looked into the apartments they passed as they walked down the hall. All of them were cold and empty inside. No sign of human life.

"I see what you mean," Siren said.

They noticed the pink wocko-bot was following them.

"Go back, wocko," Colin told the drone.

"Do you want a cheesecake?" asked the wocko-bot.

Colin was about to run it over, but Siren bumped him aside.

"Let it come," she said. "We might need it."

Colin didn't like the idea of taking a wocko along one bit.

"Fine," he said. "But if it becomes a problem we're ditching it."

When they got outside, the streets were quiet. Only the sound of rustling leaves in the wind could be heard for miles. It felt as if they were the only human beings alive.

"Which way?" Colin asked.

Siren looked down at the drone. "Wocko, how do we get to the police station?"

"Three miles north on Logan, left on Bottom for .13 mile, right on Wood for—"

"Not so loud," Colin said.

Its voice was practically yelling the directions.

The wocko-bot continued in a whisper. "One half mile, continue on Ark Street .72 mile—"

"Never mind," Siren said. "Just lead the way."

The wocko-bot twisted forward and spider-walked down the street, leading them toward the police station.

Siren scanned the area as they walked.

"Well, there's no sign of him," she said. "So far so good."

"Let's move faster," Colin said. "I want to get there as soon as we can."

A few blocks down, they saw a head rolling down the walkway, wobbling as if the man inside was drunk.

"There's somebody," Siren said, going toward the man.

When they moved in closer, they recognized the rolling face.

"He's one of the people who left the apartment building," Colin said. He pointed at the bushy eyebrows on the front of the ball. "We passed him in the hallway."

"What's he doing out here past curfew?" Siren asked.

They went to him.

"Hey, buddy, are you okay?" Siren asked.

The rolling head didn't answer. It banged into a street post. Then it backed up and went forward, banging into it again. Then again. As if he was an automated machine.

"Forget about him," Colin said.

As Siren watched the man continuously ram himself into the pole, she became flustered.

"I don't get it," she cried. "What's wrong with him?"

"Maybe he's not really human," Colin said.

"What do you mean?"

"How many people have you seen outside of their balls within the past twenty years?" Colin said. "Besides erotic dancers."

"Probably none," she said.

"Then how do you know they all have people inside?" Colin

said. "What if some bubbles are occupied by something else?"

"Like what?" Siren said.

Colin shrugged and looked at the man.

"Drones maybe," Colin said.

"Like a wocko-bot?"

Colin nodded.

Siren looked at the wocko-bot then at the silent bubble-head.

"What if way back when a lot more people died of the virus than we realized?" Colin said. "My father had said the plastic bubbles were incredibly expensive. He almost didn't bother getting one for me."

"So?"

"So what if most people couldn't afford to be saved from the virus. What if most of the population was killed off and now only a tenth of the bubbles in the world are actually filled with real people? And the rest are filled with drones."

"Why would they do something like that?" Siren asked.

"To make the world less lonely of a place," Colin said. "So that the city would seem more populated and lively."

"That's insane," Siren said. "Of course there's real people in every bubble. I've heard people talk to me. I've felt men through their plastic when I gave them lap dances."

"Then how do you explain him?" Colin said.

He pointed at the man ramming himself repeatedly into the pole. Siren shook her head when she looked at him. She didn't have an answer.

Colin said, "If you ask me, he looks like a drone that's gone defective."

The head-bubble continued ramming itself as Colin and Siren left it behind. They rolled faster to catch up to the wocko-bot that was still moving up ahead.

For the next mile, they ran into a couple more wandering heads that wouldn't speak to him. Siren was beginning to understand Colin's drone theory. The head-bubbles were spinning in circles and bouncing into walls, not reacting at all when they tried to speak to them.

As the wocko-bot led them toward the main drag that led them deep into the downtown area, Colin stopped in his tracks.

"We might not want to go this way," Colin said.

Siren looked at him. "Why?"

"Up ahead, don't you see it?" he said.

Siren examined the street more carefully. There was debris covering the area. She didn't listen to Colin's warning and followed the wocko-bot. She wanted to investigate what had happened.

The main drag looked as if a war had taken place. The road was littered with dozens of deflated plastic bubbles. Human faces flattened to the rubber road. Pools of liquid flesh leaked downhill, pouring into storm drains. Cop wagons were overturned, their lights still flashing.

"What happened here?" Siren said. "Did Kill Ball do all of this?"

"I don't know," Colin said, as they passed through the field of plastic and flesh puddles. "Bullets are useless against him, so it's possible he could kill this many people. But it seems too absurd. I think something else happened. A shootout with terrorists or something."

"There's no sign of anyone but policemen here," said Siren.

"Let's keep going," said Colin.

They entered the heart of downtown, surrounded by skyscrapers. The further into the city they went the more dead policemen they came across. There were no signs of life anywhere in the area.

"This isn't funny anymore," Siren said. "I really wish we never left the apartment."

Up ahead, a team of dead SWAT balls littered an intersection.

"Even the SWAT balls couldn't stop him?" she asked. "How? They also have bulletproof armor."

She pointed at one of the balls. It was made of a hard plastic that could stop bullets.

"I thought Kill Ball had the same kind of armor as these guys," she said.

"We don't know if it really was Kill Ball," he said. "He couldn't possibly have done all of this."

Siren pointed at a hole in the casing of the SWAT ball armor.

"Oh yes we do," she said.

It was a puncture about the size of Kill Ball's knife. Inside of the exo-armor were a deflated ball and a pool of meat juice.

Colin couldn't believe it. All of the SWAT balls seemed like they were stabbed by the same knife. The cop balls also seemed sliced open by a knife. It really was Kill Ball who did all of this. Just one man. The man who was after Siren.

"Let's get out of here," Colin said. "Fast."

Just before they turned to flee, they saw something flash in their peripheral vision. Behind them, the street lamps were going out one at a time. Not just the lamps, but the lights from the buildings. The electricity was going out block by block.

"What's causing that?" Siren asked.

The city was completely dark in that direction. But something even darker was within that darkness. A black leather ball.

"It's him," Colin said. "Let's get out of here."

And they took off, up the street, away from the darkness that was swallowing the city.

CHAPTER TEN

They ran as fast as they could, trying to escape the murderous ball. Going uphill, it didn't take much for Kill Ball to gain on them.

"Do you know the way?" Colin asked Siren as she took the lead.

They passed the wocko-bot who was moving too slow for them to worry about.

"Yeah, forget about the wocko," she said. "I know the rest of the way there." She shook her head at him. "But after seeing what he did to those SWAT balls, I have no idea how the police headquarters is going to be safe."

"It's probably a fortress," Colin said. "It's not perfect, but it's our best option."

He looked back. It was no use. Kill Ball was catching up to them too quickly.

Colin stopped in his tracks and caught his breath.

Siren looked back. "What are you doing?"

"Keep going," Colin said. "I'll hold him off."

Siren followed after him as he went in the direction of the killer.

"Are you fucking kidding me?" she yelled. "He'll destroy you."

His eyes glowed at her through his eightball bubble.

"I won't let him kill you," Colin said. "I don't care what happens to me."

Colin went for a dead SWAT ball, trying to open it so he could get inside.

Siren looked back. She didn't see the black ball in the darkness coming toward them but she knew it was in there somewhere.

"Don't be an idiot," she said.

"You're pregnant with our child," he said. "I must protect you both."

"Who said I'm pregnant?" she cried. "I don't want to have kids with you. We just met today, you freak."

"Wocko, help me," Colin called to the pink spider drone that was trying to catch up to them.

Then he turned to Siren.

"Just go," he said. "I have a plan."

Then he ordered the wocko-bot to help him open the SWAT ball casing.

"You think that's going to help you at all?" Siren said. "It didn't prevent the previous occupant from getting killed."

The wocko-bot opened the hatch and a bag of meat soup emptied into the street.

"I'm going to use it for offense, not defense," Colin said.

She couldn't waste time trying to convince him anymore. The darkness was almost around them. She was going to run with or without him.

"Trust me," he said, his glowing eye winking at her. "I'm an eightball."

Siren screamed with frustration.

"Fine, just die for nothing, asshole," she said.

Then she took off rolling down the road.

As he crawled into the armor pod, Colin looked at the black ball headed toward him. It was draining electricity out of everything so that it would become invisible in the moonless night.

"Wocko, seal me up," Colin told the pink robot.

It used four of its spindly metal legs to close up the ball and lock him inside.

"Would you like me to dance for you?" asked the wocko-bot.

"No," Colin said. "I want you to distract that man over there. He's trying to kill Siren. We have to protect her."

"Shall I go into Murder Mode?" asked the wocko-bot.

"What?"

The wocko-bot didn't explain, tilting its smiling head at him.

"There are three options for Murder Mode," said the wocko-bot. "Stabbing Mode, Lethal Injection Mode, and Flamethrower Mode."

"Flamethrower Mode?" Colin said.

"Okay," said the smiling robot. "Please hold while I murder your requested target using Flamethrower Mode."

The wocko-bot turned around and spider-walked toward the darkness.

"Why the fuck does that thing have a Murder Mode?" Colin said to himself, shaking his head.

The pink spider got into the path of Kill Ball as he came toward them. Kill Ball stopped in his tracks.

"Would you like to see me annihilate you?" asked the wocko-bot.

Then a nozzle emerged from its smiling face and shot flames into the darkness.

The pink robot's cloud of flames brightened the shadowy streets as it swallowed the Kill Ball. Colin couldn't believe it. The little robot was going to destroy the killer all on its own.

"Holy shit," he said.

Even in a bulletproof casing, nobody could survive that kind of heat. The man inside the Kill Ball would be cooked alive.

When the wocko-bot ran out of fuel, there was just a lake of fire covering the street. The rubber walkway melted and burned tar-black smoke. The trees and storefronts caught fire. Kill Ball was in the center of it all. Only a fiery sphere remained.

"Murder complete," said the wocko-bot, turning to face Colin with a smile. "Is there somebody else you'd like me to kill?"

Then a blade extended out of the fireball and pierced through the wocko-bot's pink body. Colin looked at the flames. Kill Ball was still alive in there. The blade retracted back inside and the wocko fell to the ground.

"Murder Mode backfired," said the wocko-bot, sparks spraying from the hole in its shell. "Shall I go into Heaven Mode?"

The ball of fire rolled forward, sucking the electricity out of the pink spider drone. Wocko went limp. Then the ball crushed the robot beneath him.

Colin backed away, rolling within the SWAT ball armor.

"What the fuck are you?" Colin asked the fiery bubble rolling toward him.

As it moved, its leather exterior melted and fell away, the flames smothered out against the street. What was left was not a bubble at all. It was a ball of steel.

The extendable blade darted out of the Kill Ball, aiming for Colin's bubble.

"Shit," Colin screamed.

He cartwheeled sideways, rolling out of the way. The blade retracted back into the ball. Colin was a bit surprised he survived that, but he tried to hide the amazement. He wanted to appear confident.

"I was a star pool player," Colin said. "I'm not that easy to kill."

Kill Ball seemed to nod at his words, as if taking it as a challenge.

The next time the blade extended from the steel sphere, Colin was ready for it. He kicked the side of his bubble, causing it to spin three feet to his left in an instant. The blade whizzed past him.

"Too slow," Colin said.

The metal sphere seemed to stare at him intently. The blade extended again, this time twice as fast. But it still wasn't fast enough for Colin. He spun away from it and then yawned in his direction.

"You're going to have to do better than that," Colin said.

Kill Ball tried again, extending the blade five times as fast. It was too fast even for Colin to dodge. But Colin set his ball spinning so rapidly that when the blade hit the two forces ricocheted off each other. He slid against the edge of the knife without damage, causing a screechy noise.

"I told you," Colin said. "I'm just too fast for you. Give it up and leave my Siren alone!"

Colin turned to run as the steel ball charged him. He cut across a sidewalk and turned a corner just as the blade extended. Colin laughed as his ball rotated backward. The blade flew past him across the street.

"You fell for it," Colin screamed.

Then, with all of his strength, he rammed his reinforced bubble against the pole of the extended blade, bending it against the corner of the brick building.

Once it was bent into an L-shape, Colin rolled backward and laughed at the top of his lungs.

"I got you, you son of a bitch!" he cried.

He walked backward, rolling into the center of the street, pointing at the Kill Ball, teasing him.

The steel sphere retracted the blade but it became stuck in the section where it was bent. Kill Ball could not put it back into its proper position. About fifteen feet of metal hung out of its side.

"Oh, no!" Colin said in a mocking tone. "I broke your stretchy knife!"

Kill Ball tried to roll toward Colin, but with the pole of

metal sticking out it couldn't go anywhere. The blade propped it up like a kickstand.

"Oh, you can't move either?" Colin said. "I guess you're out of luck then."

Colin turned and rolled off, laughing at the top of his lungs. The Kill Ball shifted back and forth, side to side, but no matter what it did it could not move very far with the metal in its way.

At the end of the block, just before turning the corner, Colin looked back at the Kill Ball. It struggled one last time and then stopped.

"You're finished," Colin said.

But the Kill Ball was not done yet. The metal sphere opened up.

"What the hell?"

Clockwork gears spun and twisted within the insides of the ball as it unfolded like a mechanical puzzle. Colin could hear ticking noises as the clockwork pieces of the sphere rotated and reorganized. A circular saw emerged from the inner gears, creating a ring around the sphere. It resembled a steel version of the planet Saturn.

"You're a machine," Colin said. "Who the hell built you?"

The saw whizzed to life, creating a shrieking noise that echoed through the streets as it cut through the bent pole of metal stuck to its side. It wouldn't be long before the Kill Ball was back in action.

"I'm sorry, my love," Colin said. "I wasn't able to stop him."

Then he turned around and rolled deeper into the city, hoping to catch up to Siren before the Kill Ball could.

94

CHAPTER ELEVEN

On the way to the police headquarters, Colin combed the streets in search of Siren. She was nowhere to be seen. He hoped she was already at the station, already safe.

He couldn't see the Kill Ball coming after him, but he could hear him out there somewhere. The sound of a whirring circular saw cutting the sidewalk echoed through the buildings.

The strobing lights of a cop ball flashed from around a corner. Colin followed it. The police siren wasn't turned on, but the lights flashed continuously.

The cop ball was rolling slowly through the streets. Based on its wobbly movements, the man inside seemed to be toppling over with each step it took.

"Hey," Colin said, approaching the bubble.

The cop ball continued wobbling.

"Did you come from the fight back there?" Colin asked. "I saw all the bodies. Everyone's dead."

The cop didn't say anything, just rolling.

"But you survived?" he asked. "What happened?"

No response.

"I'm looking for a woman," Colin said. "Did she come by here? She was on the way to police headquarters. She wasn't wearing any clothes."

No response.

Colin tried to look through the plastic. He couldn't see anyone inside of there. Just the lights.

"So you're one of them, are you?" Colin said.

He bumped him with his bubble. He couldn't get any reaction out of him.

"What the hell are you people really?" he asked. "Are you a

drone? Has Kill Ball's jamming mechanism messed up your circuits, caused you to go haywire?"

Colin bumped him again. The cop ball bumped him back. Colin rolled away a few feet.

"Wait," Colin said. "Is there really somebody in there? Hello?"

He bumped him. The cop ball bumped him back.

Colin followed the ball back toward police headquarters. He searched around, but Siren wasn't there. At least, not in front.

Outside of the entrance, the wobbling cop ball went toward three more bubble-heads rolling in circles. Colin approached them.

"Have any of you seen a woman come through here?" he asked them.

None of them answered. A bald bubble-head with glasses rolled over to Colin, as if to speak to him. His giant face shifted forward.

"Have you seen her?" he asked.

The bubble-head didn't respond.

"What's wrong?" Colin asked.

He couldn't hear it clearly, but somewhere deep down inside of the ball he heard the man say something. He repeated one word over and over again. In a squeaky, barely-audible, whispering voice, the bubble-head said, "Help."

"Help?" Colin asked. "What's wrong?"

"Heeeelp," whispered the man in the ball.

Before he even saw it coming, Colin heard Kill Ball fly across the street. It was propped up on its side, using the circular saw like a wheel, rolling at high speed through the rubber road.

"Look out," Colin said to the crowd of bubble-heads.

They did nothing to flee. Kill Ball sliced through them, tearing into them in the blink of an eye. But the bubbles did not pop.

Colin fell backward when he saw it. The bubble with the

bald man's face stayed intact, even though it had been halved.

Kill Ball continued down the street, taking a wide turn before coming back at them.

Colin used the moment to investigate the victims. One half of bald-head was lying flat on the street. The other half was face up. Inside the bubble was something not human.

"What are you?" Colin asked the bubble half.

The entire bubble was filled with meat and bones. The flesh was strings of muscle that were connected to the insides of the plastic casing. He could make out lungs, a heart, and intestines. The insides of the ball were similar to the insides of a human. Colin was expecting them to be filled with drones, not muscle and organs.

The Kill Ball took another pass at Colin and he spun out of the way. Kill Ball slashed through another bubble-head. Blood sprayed across the road in a giant gush.

Inside the new victim, Colin saw the same meat as the bald-bubble. Only this one didn't just have meat inside. There was also a human face. It was stretched and distorted, but it was definitely human.

The face looked at Colin as it died.

"Heeelp me," said the face inside the ball, just before its flesh melted across the sidewalk.

Seeing the human-like creature inside the ball made Colin realize what was happening. They were mutating. Like Siren and Colin, all of these weird balls were rapidly evolving into a new species of human. Only instead of evolving to leave their bubbles, these people were evolving to become a part of them.

Colin bounced over the ball-shaped corpses and rolled up the ramp to the police station. In the background, Kill Ball was tearing through the rubber toward him.

"Out of the way," Colin yelled to the sluggish bubble-heads rolling around the entrance.

He slammed through them, knocking them back, to force his way within. Once inside, he shut the door and rammed into the button that reinforced the lock. Kill Ball smashed into the outside of the door, but couldn't break through it by force. It had to cut through.

Colin looked around the police lobby, ignoring the shrieking sound of the saw outside the door. He prayed Siren was already inside. If she didn't make it to the headquarters in time, all would be lost.

Colin rolled through the building, yelling out Siren's name.

"Has anyone seen her?" Colin asked the police officers rolling through the halls.

But none of them spoke to him. They were all mutating. All were transforming into ball people.

He went up a floor and searched that area. Then he went up to the next floor. Siren didn't seem to be there.

"Siren, are you here?"

He couldn't find her anywhere.

By the time he made it to the top floor, his hope of reuniting with the woman he loved was wearing thin. He knew she didn't want to go to the police station, so where would she have gone? Back home? Back to the club she worked at?

"Colin," said a voice from a back office.

It wasn't Siren's voice. The sound was deep and loud. The voice of an angry God.

"Colin Hinchcliff, is that you?" repeated the voice.

Colin followed the sound of the voice into the office.

"Detective Park?" Colin said, when he saw the Asian bubble-head looking at him from behind a desk.

"Yes, it's me," said the detective in a loud booming voice.

When he spoke, the sound didn't come from a human inside the bubble. He was speaking from the giant mouth on the ball itself.

"What happened to you?" Colin asked.

The tiny hand on the side of the ball, the one that was used to fire weapons, pulled on the sunglasses painted on its face. The hand peeled away the sunglasses, just strips of black plastic, and revealed two giant bulbous eyes.

The monstrous eyeballs rolled around in their sockets and then stared at Colin. The detective was a mutant like the others, only his evolution was complete. He was what the other ball-humans were becoming—a giant living rolling head.

"Are you an outie or an innie?" asked the detective.

Colin shrugged. "What do you mean?"

"Which way have you transformed?" he asked, his lips the size of human legs. "Did you mutate outward like the dancers or inward like everyone else?"

"Outward," Colin said.

"Good," said the giant head. "They won't be very pleased to know you live, but I'm happy to hear that."

"Who do you mean by they?" Colin asked.

"The people who sent Kill Ball after your woman," said Park. "They were trying to stop your species from evolving."

The giant head rolled out from behind the desk toward Colin. It closed its eyes as it rolled over its own face to get across the floor.

"We knew it was going to happen," Park said, rolling upright and facing Colin. "But we had no idea how fast it would come. We thought we still had a few decades. I wonder if somebody out there discovered a way to speed up the process…"

The giant head rolled around Colin, as if pacing the room. A small meaty ball squirted out of a hole in the back of the detective's head as he moved. The hole looked similar to an anus.

"Pardon me," said the giant head, as if he had just farted.

Colin looked down at the ball of meat, wondering if he had just taken a dump on the floor.

"It will be better for our future to have you around," said the giant head.

Colin was so close to him that he could make out the details of his face more clearly. The eyes were big and bulgy, horrifying and cartoonish. Its exterior was no longer plastic, but sweaty, hairy flesh.

"But the Kill Ball must be stopped if you want to survive," said the giant head. "And I have no idea how you will accomplish this. Kill Ball was designed to be the ultimate killing machine."

"I thought you were trying to stop it," Colin said.

"I was," said the head. "I didn't want it to destroy your race. But now I have too many things to do."

He rolled back toward the desk. Another ball of meat plopped out of his backside.

"There is a new future ahead of my people," said the creature that was once Detective Park. "I must make sure that we flourish. You should do the same. If you can stop the Kill Ball your people will need a leader. Somebody brave."

Colin noticed the balls of meat that had fallen from the detective were shifting.

"I've lost Siren," Colin said. "She was supposed to come here, as you asked us to. But I can't find her."

"She came and left," said the giant head.

"You saw her?" Colin asked.

"No," he said. "But some of my people saw her downstairs. We can see through each other's eyes now. Our minds are linked together. We think as one."

"Do you know where she went?" Colin asked.

"Yes, I do," said the giant head. "As a matter of fact, one of my people can see her at this very moment. She is leaving the downtown area, heading east. I believe she is trying to get across the river, to flee town."

"She must have assumed I had been killed already," Colin said.

"Hurry," said the creature's booming voice. "If you want to save her you must hurry."

Colin agreed. He was going to save her no matter what.

As he rolled toward the door, he saw one of the small lumps of meat turning over. On its side was a human face. It began to cry. The other lump of meat also began to cry, rolling across the room.

"What are they?" Colin asked the giant head.

"They're my babies," he said.

His grotesque lips curled into a smile.

"Unlike your people," said the giant head, "my species reproduces asexually. Because sex had become an impossibility for humans, this was a natural solution."

Colin just stared at the squirming little heads that rolled across the detective's office. Although the creatures were infants, they did not have the faces of babies. They were the faces of grown men.

CHAPTER TWELVE

As Colin went downstairs, he saw many giant heads rolling casually through the offices. A lot of the ball-people had already finished their evolution. A giant female head with long curly blond hair rolled sideways down the hallway. Two bald males bumped into each other and then laughed with deep growling chuckles.

"Watch it," they said to each other with their ogre-like voices. "I'm rolling here."

Several baby head balls bounced across Colin's path making squeaky gurgle noises.

"Am I the only one here still in a plastic bubble?" Colin asked.

He was a little jealous of them. Even though they were grotesque head-creatures, at least they were no longer in danger of melting upon contact with the air. They could see and touch each other, while Colin was still stuck in his ball.

"Look out," Colin said to a group of baby heads hopping up and down in front of him.

They didn't seem to understand language yet. He had to bonk them out of the way to get by.

On the next floor down, he heard the head-people yelling in their deep voices.

"Look out," they bellowed at each other.

Then Colin saw it. The Kill Ball was inside, tearing the place apart.

One giant head pulled a gun out with its single tiny arm and fired at the steel ball.

"Get down, fucker," said the giant head.

Kill Ball opened its body outward and a long sickle swung out of it, slicing the head down the middle. Blood sprayed across the walls.

When the steel machine spotted Colin, it sped through the hall toward him. Colin rolled back the way he came. The head people fired pistols at the intruder, but the bullets only bounced off of its metal frame.

"He's bulletproof," Colin told the giant heads. "You need something armor-piercing."

Colin looked back to see Kill Ball running over the bouncing baby heads that crossed its path, smooshing them like wine grapes against the linoleum floor. The sickle pointed out of the sphere slashed at the eightball as it gained on him.

When he reached the end of the hallway, Colin only had one place left to go. He leapt from the ground and smashed through the window, plummeting through the air.

Colin woke up on another side of town. After jumping from the window, he had hit the ground hard enough to break the exterior SWAT ball armor, knocking him out in the process. Then his ball bounced him high over the buildings, ricocheting off of walls and rolling down streets. It was like Colin was one of those super bouncy balls he used to play with as a kid. If he hadn't been within a flexible eightball designed for extreme sports, Colin wouldn't have survived.

He was blocks away from the police station, but he didn't know how long he had been out. It could have only been a few seconds or it could have been several minutes, maybe even hours. He had no idea how far away he was from Kill Ball. Hopefully, his pursuer had lost him completely.

The morning sun brightened the cityscape. The roads began to fill with giant rolling heads, all of them made of meat instead of plastic, coming out of their buildings as if on their way to work. They spoke to each other in their deep voices, greeting each other and making small talk, but Colin was too focused on his mission to listen to what they were saying.

He went toward the outskirts of town, where Detective Park said Siren was headed. They would escape the city together, flee those who wanted to put an end to their species, and live happily ever after as shiny blue mates.

He saw her on the bridge up ahead, crossing the river. Seeing the beautiful blue tattoos on her naked flesh put a smile on his face. But what he was really looking forward to was seeing the blue flesh hidden beneath those tattoos.

"Siren," Colin yelled to her as she reached the center of the bridge. "Siren!"

She turned around. Her eyes lit up when she saw him rolling toward her. She blushed in disbelief.

"My name's not Siren," she yelled back at him.

Then she laughed.

Colin didn't understand *Siren* was only her stage name as a dancer.

She rolled toward him as he rolled toward the bridge. The second their balls collided, he planned to leap out of his skin, wrap himself around her, and kiss her with everything he had.

But before she got to the edge of the bridge, she stopped short. Then she backed away. Colin looked to his side. Kill Ball was rolling toward her from another direction, getting between them.

"No," Colin yelled.

He rolled as fast as he could, trying to grab the ball's attention, but he was still too far away. Kill Ball was almost on her.

"Get away from her," Colin screamed.

The steel ball opened and the sickle blade launched out, sliced into Siren's bubble. The cold metal impaled her through the chest.

"Siren," Colin cried, repeating her name as loud as he could.

But he was too late. Her plastic bubble had fallen apart. Her flesh was beginning to melt. There was no life left in her eyes.

Colin's despair quickly turned to rage.

"You're fucking dead, motherfucker," Colin screamed at the ball, charging toward it at full speed.

When his bubble slammed into Kill Ball, Colin leapt outside of his body, through his plastic skin, and deep into the steel of the murderous machine.

"You're dead, you're dead, you're dead," Colin cried.

His glowing blue flesh seeped through the steel casing until it arrived at the heart of the ball. But he was taken aback when he saw two faces staring back at him.

"Get away," the two faces cried, hissing at him in unison.

The Kill Ball wasn't a drone as Colin expected. Inside the machine, there was a pilot. It was a two-headed creature, twins who were conjoined into one being.

"Get out of my body," the faces hissed. "Get out of me."

They tried to push at Colin with their miniature hands, but their limbs only fell through his glowing flesh.

The twins were once human, but hardly looked it. They were adults the size of infants. They had been inserted into Kill Ball when they were only babies and had grown into the machinery. Their flesh was not only conjoined together, but also conjoined with their machine.

"You killed her," Colin screamed at them.

He was like a blue giant inside of there with them.

They used their tiny limbs to move levers, flip switches, trying everything to get Colin to leave their insides. His presence sent them into a panic.

"You killed her!"

Colin inserted his shining hand inside of the conjoined freaks' chest. The creature shrieked and moaned, slapping at his wrist.

"I will fucking destroy you," Colin yelled.

He pulled his hand out of their chest, ripping something

out with it. In his palm, a tiny blue glowing heart pumped within his fingers. The arteries snapped and Colin tore it free, shimmering blood gushed across the inner cavity of the ball. The twins shrieked, clutching at their chest, trying to retrieve what the intruder had stolen.

The twins coughed and wheezed. Then they died.

Colin dropped his face against their conjoined corpse. Kill Ball was finally dead.

When Colin pulled himself out of Kill Ball, he tried to re-enter his body but found it to be impossible. The ball's sickle weapon had ruptured his bubble and decapitated the human head from his body.

Colin just watched as his body melted in front of him. He was dying. His blue mouth hung open as he watched himself liquefying in the same way he saw his poor mother liquefy as a child.

But once the meat was soft and soggy, Colin found he was able to slide his blue feet all the way out of the flesh. His blue form could stand on its own, outside of his bubble, without the need of his old body.

"You did it," said a woman's voice behind him. "You killed him."

Colin turned to see Siren standing there in her shiny inner flesh, kicking the steel ball.

"You're alive?" Colin cried.

Siren smiled at him.

"I jumped out of my skin just before he got me," Siren said. "It must have been a survival reflex."

"Will we survive like this?" Colin asked. "I thought we needed our old bodies."

Siren shrugged. "I don't think we need them anymore. We've evolved beyond our old flesh."

She came to Colin, looked him in his ghostly eyes. Then she wrapped her arms around him and pulled him close.

"We did it," she said. "We escaped."

They crossed over the bridge, holding each other closely. Siren laid her cheek on his shoulder as they passed rolling heads going in the opposite direction. She didn't need to ask him what the giant heads were. She had already figured it out.

On the other side of the river, they discovered more people of their kind—glowing blue couples smiling at each other and rubbing each other's new skin. Siren recognized many of her friends among them, dancers who had escaped their bodies during the night. They welcomed her with kisses on her nose.

The human race ended that day, but from its remains there birthed two new species: the heads and the blues. Whether the two peoples would become mortal enemies of each other or find a way to live together in peace nobody could foresee. All that was certain was that the two species would never be one again.

"Now what do we do?" Colin asked Siren, as their blue flesh sparkled in the water under the bridge.

"Now we build our new world," Siren responded.

Then she kissed him in a way that no human being had been kissed in a very, very long time.

BONUS SECTION

This is the part of the book where we would have published an afterword by the author but he insisted on drawing a comic strip instead for reasons we don't quite understand.

I hope you enjoyed my new book, *Kill Ball.* Wasn't it exciting?

It's me CM3!

MEET THE AUTHOR

Kill Ball

Kill Ball

IT SUCKED!!!

bitter douchebag newbie writer

why is his arm part of his head?

But I tried my best...

I wrote better books when I was 5 years old.

M C TACO

I kicked off heads better when I was 5 years old!

nunchucks

MC Taco

Hmm... Maybe I shouldn't have kicked his head off... I'm kind of sad now...

decapitated

Sure he was a bitter douchebag who unfairly attacked my work, but it was only because he was a new writer. Trashing the work of more successful writers is what all new writers do in order to cope with the frustration of constantly being rejected by publishers...

I was exactly the same way when I was a new writer...

Thanks for coming to my book signing. I'm Dean Koontz.

Young douchebag CM3

MEET DEAN KOONTZ

You suck!!!

But I try my best...

Dean Koontz used to have an awesome mustache

What a loser! You don't even have a single flesh-eating tank in any of your books!

Fact: the quality of a work of literature is determined by the number of flesh-eating tanks that appear in the story.

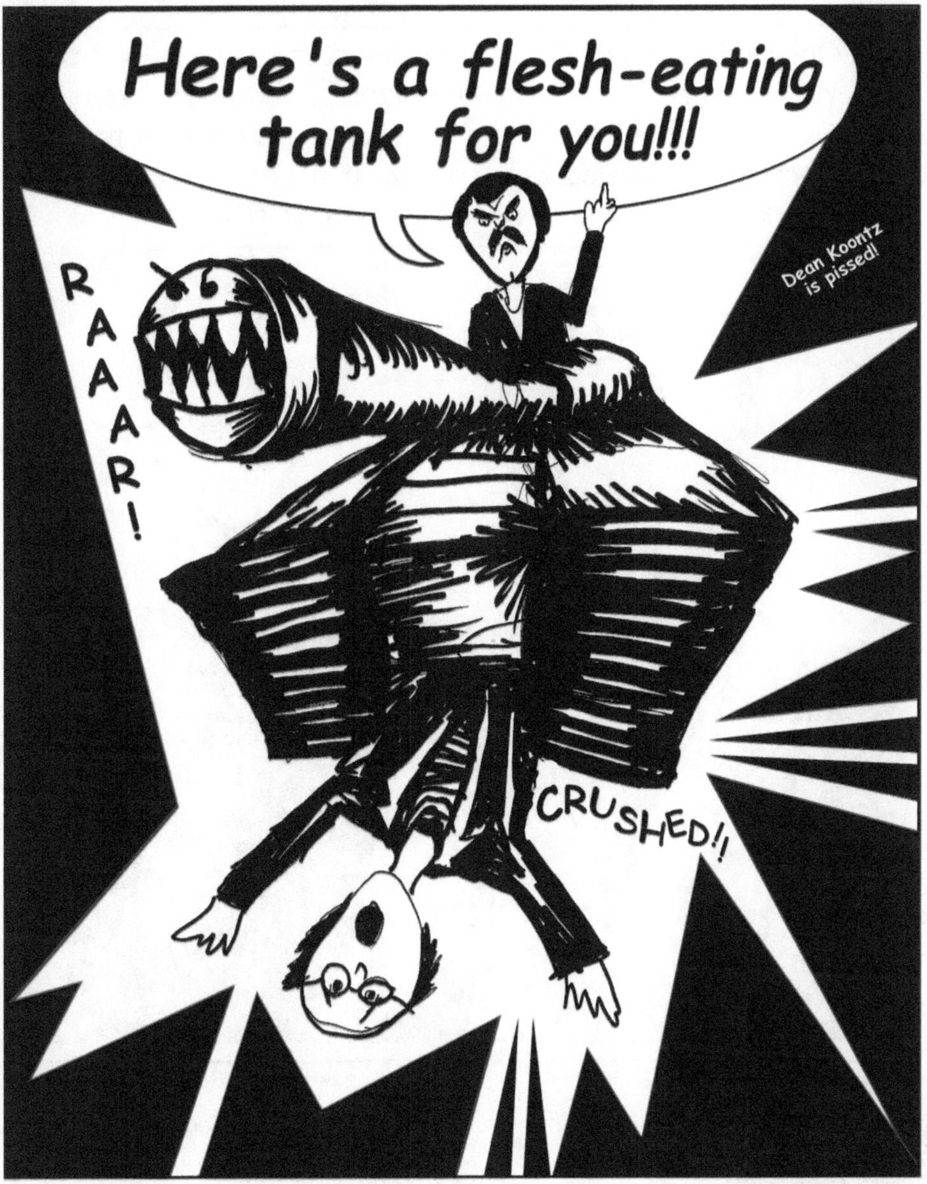

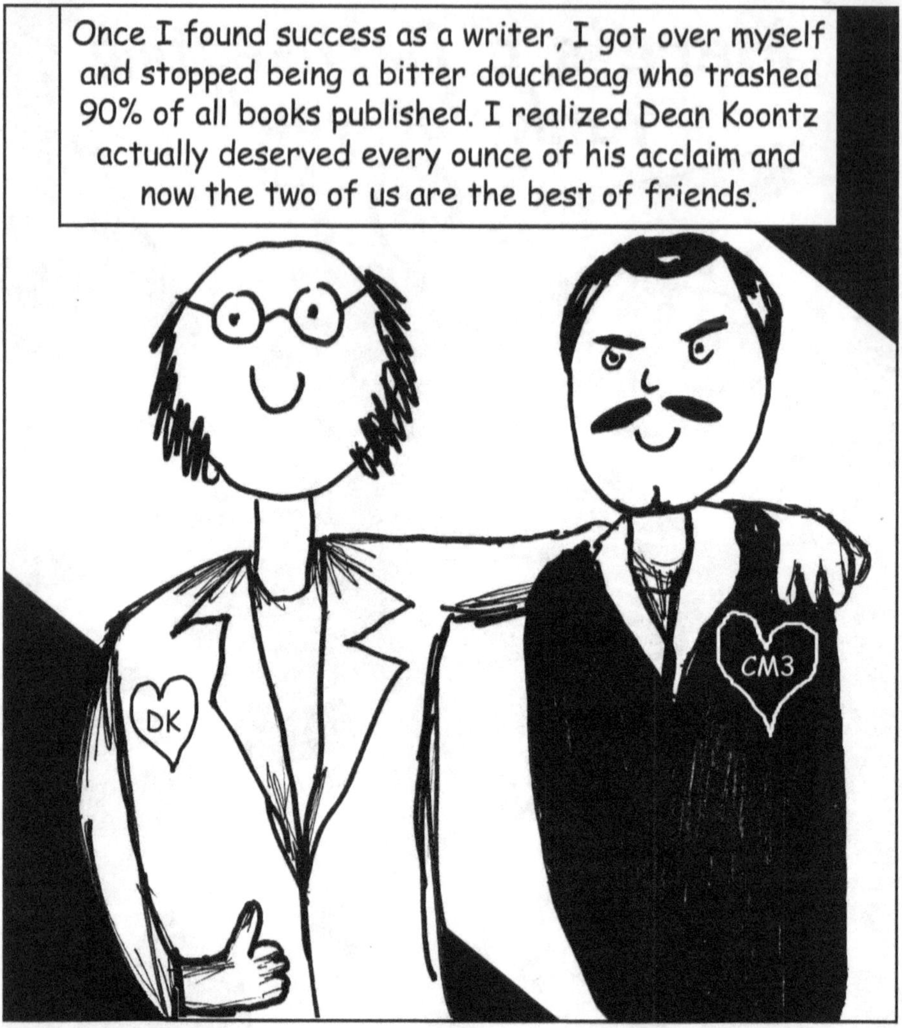

Once I found success as a writer, I got over myself and stopped being a bitter douchebag who trashed 90% of all books published. I realized Dean Koontz actually deserved every ounce of his acclaim and now the two of us are the best of friends.

BULLSHIT!! He doesn't even know you exist!

He stapled his head back on.

ABOUT THE AUTHOR

Carlton Mellick III is one of the leading authors of the bizarro fiction subgenre. Since 2001, his books have drawn an international cult following, despite the fact that they have been shunned by most libraries and chain bookstores.

He won the Wonderland Book Award for his novel, *Warrior Wolf Women of the Wasteland*, in 2009. His short fiction has appeared in *Vice Magazine, The Year's Best Fantasy and Horror #16, The Magazine of Bizarro Fiction,* and *Zombies: Encounters with the Hungry Dead*, among others. He is also a graduate of Clarion West, where he studied under the likes of Chuck Palahniuk, Connie Willis, and Cory Doctorow.

He lives in Portland, OR, the bizarro fiction mecca.

Visit him online at **www.carltonmellick.com**

Bizarro Books

CATALOG   SPRING 2012

ERASERHEAD PRESS

Your major resource for the bizarro fiction genre:

WWW.BIZARROCENTRAL.COM

Introduce yourselves to the bizarro fiction genre and all of its authors with the Bizarro Starter Kit series. Each volume features short novels and short stories by ten of the leading bizarro authors, designed to give you a perfect sampling of the genre for only $10.

BB-0X1
"The Bizarro Starter Kit"
(Orange)
Featuring D. Harlan Wilson, Carlton Mellick III, Jeremy Robert Johnson, Kevin L Donihe, Gina Ranalli, Andre Duza, Vincent W. Sakowski, Steve Beard, John Edward Lawson, and Bruce Taylor.
236 pages $10

BB-0X2
"The Bizarro Starter Kit"
(Blue)
Featuring Ray Fracalossy, Jeremy C. Shipp, Jordan Krall, Mykle Hansen, Andersen Prunty, Eckhard Gerdes, Bradley Sands, Steve Aylett, Christian TeBordo, and Tony Rauch. **244 pages $10**

BB-0X2
"The Bizarro Starter Kit"
(Purple)
Featuring Russell Edson, Athena Villaverde, David Agranoff, Matthew Revert, Andrew Goldfarb, Jeff Burk, Garrett Cook, Kris Saknussemm, Cody Goodfellow, and Cameron Pierce **264 pages $10**

BB-001 "The Kafka Effekt" D. Harlan Wilson — A collection of forty-four irreal short stories loosely written in the vein of Franz Kafka, with more than a pinch of William S. Burroughs sprinkled on top. **211 pages $14**

BB-002 "Satan Burger" Carlton Mellick III — The cult novel that put Carlton Mellick III on the map ... Six punks get jobs at a fast food restaurant owned by the devil in a city violently overpopulated by surreal alien cultures. **236 pages $14**

BB-003 "Some Things Are Better Left Unplugged" Vincent Sakwoski — Join The Man and his Nemesis, the obese tabby, for a nightmare roller coaster ride into this postmodern fantasy. **152 pages $10**

BB-004 "Shall We Gather At the Garden?" Kevin L Donihe — Donihe's Debut novel. Midgets take over the world, The Church of Lionel Richie vs. The Church of the Byrds, plant porn and more! **244 pages $14**

BB-005 "Razor Wire Pubic Hair" Carlton Mellick III — A genderless humandildo is purchased by a razor dominatrix and brought into her nightmarish world of bizarre sex and mutilation. **176 pages $11**

BB-006 "Stranger on the Loose" D. Harlan Wilson — The fiction of Wilson's 2nd collection is planted in the soil of normalcy, but what grows out of that soil is a dark, witty, otherworldly jungle... **228 pages $14**

BB-007 "The Baby Jesus Butt Plug" Carlton Mellick III — Using clones of the Baby Jesus for anal sex will be the hip sex fetish of the future. **92 pages $10**

BB-008 "Fishyfleshed" Carlton Mellick III — The world of the past is an illogical flatland lacking in dimension and color, a sick-scape of crispy squid people wandering the desert for no apparent reason. **260 pages $14**

BB-009 **"Dead Bitch Army" Andre Duza** — Step into a world filled with racist teenagers, cannibals, 100 warped Uncle Sams, automobiles with razor-sharp teeth, living graffiti, and a pissed-off zombie bitch out for revenge. **344 pages $16**

BB-010 **"The Menstruating Mall" Carlton Mellick III** — "The Breakfast Club meets Chopping Mall as directed by David Lynch." - Brian Keene **212 pages $12**

BB-011 **"Angel Dust Apocalypse" Jeremy Robert Johnson** — Meth-heads, man-made monsters, and murderous Neo-Nazis. "Seriously amazing short stories..." - Chuck Palahniuk, author of Fight Club **184 pages $11**

BB-012 **"Ocean of Lard" Kevin L Donihe / Carlton Mellick III** — A parody of those old Choose Your Own Adventure kid's books about some very odd pirates sailing on a sea made of animal fat. **176 pages $12**

BB-015 **"Foop!" Chris Genoa** — Strange happenings are going on at Dactyl, Inc, the world's first and only time travel tourism company. "A surreal pie in the face!" - Christopher Moore **300 pages $14**

BB-020 **"Punk Land" Carlton Mellick III** — In the punk version of Heaven, the anarchist utopia is threatened by corporate fascism and only Goblin, Mortician's sperm, and a blue-mohawked female assassin named Shark Girl can stop them. **284 pages $15**

BB-027 **"Siren Promised" Jeremy Robert Johnson & Alan M Clark** — Nominated for the Bram Stoker Award. A potent mix of bad drugs, bad dreams, brutal bad guys, and surreal/incredible art by Alan M. Clark. **190 pages $13**

BB-031 **"Sea of the Patchwork Cats" Carlton Mellick III** — A quiet dreamlike tale set in the ashes of the human race. For Mellick enthusiasts who also adore The Twilight Zone. **112 pages $10**

BB-032 "Extinction Journals" Jeremy Robert Johnson — An uncanny voyage across a newly nuclear America where one man must confront the problems associated with loneliness, insane dieties, radiation, love, and an ever-evolving cockroach suit with a mind of its own. **104 pages $10**

BB-037 "The Haunted Vagina" Carlton Mellick III — It's difficult to love a woman whose vagina is a gateway to the world of the dead. **132 pages $10**

BB-043 "War Slut" Carlton Mellick III — Part "1984," part "Waiting for Godot," and part action horror video game adaptation of John Carpenter's "The Thing." **116 pages $10**

BB-047 "Sausagey Santa" Carlton Mellick III — A bizarro Christmas tale featuring Santa as a piratey mutant with a body made of sausages. 124 pages $10

BB-048 "Misadventures in a Thumbnail Universe" Vincent Sakowski — Dive deep into the surreal and satirical realms of neo-classical Blender Fiction, filled with television shoes and flesh-filled skies. **120 pages $10**

BB-053 "Ballad of a Slow Poisoner" Andrew Goldfarb — Millford Mutterwurst sat down on a Tuesday to take his afternoon tea, and made the unpleasant discovery that his elbows were becoming flatter. **128 pages $10**

BB-055 "Help! A Bear is Eating Me" Mykle Hansen — The bizarro, heartwarming, magical tale of poor planning, hubris and severe blood loss... **150 pages $11**

BB-056 "Piecemeal June" Jordan Krall — A man falls in love with a living sex doll, but with love comes danger when her creator comes after her with crab-squid assassins. **90 pages $9**

BB-058 "The Overwhelming Urge" Andersen Prunty — A collection of bizarro tales by Andersen Prunty. **150 pages $11**

BB-059 "Adolf in Wonderland" Carlton Mellick III — A dreamlike adventure that takes a young descendant of Adolf Hitler's design and sends him down the rabbit hole into a world of imperfection and disorder. **180 pages $11**

BB-061 "Ultra Fuckers" Carlton Mellick III — Absurdist suburban horror about a couple who enter an upper middle class gated community but can't find their way out. **108 pages $9**

BB-062 "House of Houses" Kevin L. Donihe — An odd man wants to marry his house. Unfortunately, all of the houses in the world collapse at the same time in the Great House Holocaust. Now he must travel to House Heaven to find his departed fiancee. **172 pages $11**

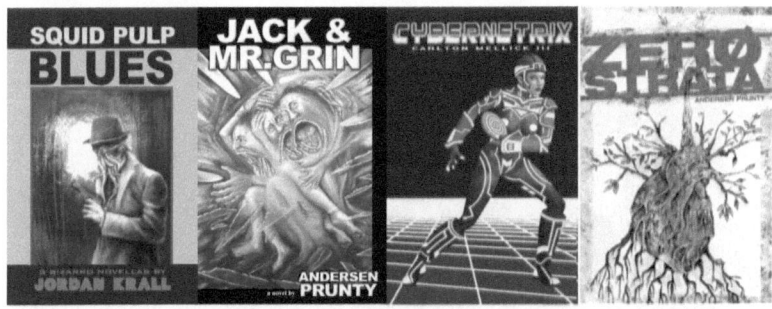

BB-064 "Squid Pulp Blues" Jordan Krall — In these three bizarro-noir novellas, the reader is thrown into a world of murderers, drugs made from squid parts, deformed gun-toting veterans, and a mischievous apocalyptic donkey. **204 pages $12**

BB-065 "Jack and Mr. Grin" Andersen Prunty — "When Mr. Grin calls you can hear a smile in his voice. Not a warm and friendly smile, but the kind that seizes your spine in fear. You don't need to pay your phone bill to hear it. That smile is in every line of Prunty's prose." - Tom Bradley. **208 pages $12**

BB-066 "Cybernetrix" Carlton Mellick III — What would you do if your normal everyday world was slowly mutating into the video game world from Tron? **212 pages $12**

BB-072 "Zerostrata" Andersen Prunty — Hansel Nothing lives in a tree house, suffers from memory loss, has a very eccentric family, and falls in love with a woman who runs naked through the woods every night. **144 pages $11**

BB-073 "The Egg Man" Carlton Mellick III — It is a world where humans reproduce like insects. Children are the property of corporations, and having an enormous ten-foot brain implanted into your skull is a grotesque sexual fetish. Mellick's industrial urban dystopia is one of his darkest and grittiest to date. **184 pages $11**

BB-074 "Shark Hunting in Paradise Garden" Cameron Pierce — A group of strange humanoid religious fanatics travel back in time to the Garden of Eden to discover it is invested with hundreds of giant flying maneating sharks. **150 pages $10**

BB-075 "Apeshit" Carlton Mellick III - Friday the 13th meets Visitor Q. Six hipster teens go to a cabin in the woods inhabited by a deformed killer. An incredibly fucked-up parody of B-horror movies with a bizarro slant. **192 pages $12**

BB-076 "Fuckers of Everything on the Crazy Shitting Planet of the Vomit At smosphere" Mykle Hansen - Three bizarro satires. Monster Cocks, Journey to the Center of Agnes Cuddlebottom, and Crazy Shitting Planet. **228 pages $12**

BB-077 "The Kissing Bug" Daniel Scott Buck — In the tradition of Roald Dahl, Tim Burton, and Edward Gorey, comes this bizarro anti-war children's story about a bohemian conenose kissing bug who falls in love with a human woman. **116 pages $10**

BB-078 "MachoPoni" Lotus Rose — It's My Little Pony... *Bizarro* style! A long time ago Poniworld was split in two. On one side of the Jagged Line is the Pastel Kingdom, a magical land of music, parties, and positivity. On the other side of the Jagged Line is Dark Kingdom inhabited by an army of undead ponies. **148 pages $11**

BB-079 "The Faggiest Vampire" Carlton Mellick III — A Roald Dahlesque children's story about two faggy vampires who partake in a mustache competition to find out which one is truly the faggiest. **104 pages $10**

BB-080 "Sky Tongues" Gina Ranalli — The autobiography of Sky Tongues, the biracial hermaphrodite actress with tongues for fingers. Follow her strange life story as she rises from freak to fame. **204 pages $12**

BB-081 **"Washer Mouth" Kevin L. Donihe** - A washing machine becomes human and pursues his dream of meeting his favorite soap opera star. **244 pages $11**

BB-082 **"Shatnerquake" Jeff Burk** - All of the characters ever played by William Shatner are suddenly sucked into our world. Their mission: hunt down and destroy the real William Shatner. **100 pages $10**

BB-083 **"The Cannibals of Candyland" Carlton Mellick III** - There exists a race of cannibals that are made of candy. They live in an underground world made out of candy. One man has dedicated his life to killing them all. **170 pages $11**

BB-084 **"Slub Glub in the Weird World of the Weeping Willows"** **Andrew Goldfarb** - The charming tale of a blue glob named Slub Glub who helps the weeping willows whose tears are flooding the earth. There are also hyenas, ghosts, and a voodoo priest **100 pages $10**

BB-085 **"Super Fetus" Adam Pepper** - Try to abort this fetus and he'll kick your ass! **104 pages $10**

BB-086 **"Fistful of Feet" Jordan Krall** - A bizarro tribute to spaghetti westerns, featuring Cthulhu-worshipping Indians, a woman with four feet, a crazed gunman who is obsessed with sucking on candy, Syphilis-ridden mutants, sexually transmitted tattoos, and a house devoted to the freakiest fetishes. **228 pages $12**

BB-087 **"Ass Goblins of Auschwitz" Cameron Pierce** - It's Monty Python meets Nazi exploitation in a surreal nightmare as can only be imagined by Bizarro author Cameron Pierce. **104 pages $10**

BB-088 **"Silent Weapons for Quiet Wars" Cody Goodfellow** - "This is high-end psychological surrealist horror meets bottom-feeding low-life crime in a techno-thrilling science fiction world full of Lovecraft and magic..." -John Skipp **212 pages $12**

BB-089 "Warrior Wolf Women of the Wasteland" Carlton Mellick III
— Road Warrior Werewolves versus McDonaldland Mutants...post-apocalyptic fiction has never been quite like this. **316 pages $13**

BB-091 "Super Giant Monster Time" Jeff Burk — A tribute to choose your own adventures and Godzilla movies. Will you escape the giant monsters that are rampaging the fuck out of your city and shit? Or will you join the mob of alien-controlled punk rockers causing chaos in the streets? What happens next depends on you. **188 pages $12**

BB-092 "Perfect Union" Cody Goodfellow — "Cronenberg's THE FLY on a grand scale: human/insect gene-spliced body horror, where the human hive politics are as shocking as the gore." -John Skipp. **272 pages $13**

BB-093 "Sunset with a Beard" Carlton Mellick III — 14 stories of surreal science fiction. **200 pages $12**

BB-094 "My Fake War" Andersen Prunty — The absurd tale of an unlikely soldier forced to fight a war that, quite possibly, does not exist. It's Rambo meets Waiting for Godot in this subversive satire of American values and the scope of the human imagination. **128 pages $11**

BB-095 "Lost in Cat Brain Land" Cameron Pierce — Sad stories from a surreal world. A fascist mustache, the ghost of Franz Kafka, a desert inside a dead cat. Primordial entities mourn the death of their child. The desperate serve tea to mysterious creatures. A hopeless romantic falls in love with a pterodactyl. And much more. **152 pages $11**

BB-096 "The Kobold Wizard's Dildo of Enlightenment +2" Carlton Mellick III — A Dungeons and Dragons parody about a group of people who learn they are only made up characters in an AD&D campaign and must find a way to resist their nerdy teenaged players and retarded dungeon master in order to survive. **232 pages $12**

BB-098 "A Hundred Horrible Sorrows of Ogner Stump" Andrew Goldfarb — Goldfarb's acclaimed comic series. A magical and weird journey into the horrors of everyday life. **164 pages $11**

BB-099 "Pickled Apocalypse of Pancake Island" Cameron Pierce—A demented fairy tale about a pickle, a pancake, and the apocalypse. **102 pages $8**

BB-100 "Slag Attack" Andersen Prunty— Slag Attack features four visceral, noir stories about the living, crawling apocalypse.A slag is what survivors are calling the slug-like maggots raining from the sky, burrowing inside people, and hollowing out their flesh and their sanity. **148 pages $11**

BB-101 "Slaughterhouse High" Robert Devereaux—A place where schools are built with secret passageways, rebellious teens get zippers installed in their mouths and genitals, and once a year, on that special night, one couple is slaughtered and the bits of their bodies are kept as souvenirs. **304 pages $13**

BB-102 "The Emerald Burrito of Oz" John Skipp & Marc Levinthal —OZ IS REAL! Magic is real! The gate is really in Kansas! And America is finally allowing Earth tourists to visit this weird-ass, mysterious land. But when Gene of Los Angeles heads off for summer vacation in the Emerald City, little does he know that a war is brewing...a war that could destroy both worlds. **280 pages $13**

BB-103 "The Vegan Revolution... with Zombies" David Agranoff — When there's no more meat in hell, the vegans will walk the earth. **160 pages $11**

BB-104 "The Flappy Parts" Kevin L Donihe—Poems about bunnies, LSD, and police abuse. You know, things that matter. 132 **pages $11**

BB-105 "Sorry I Ruined Your Orgy" Bradley Sands—Bizarro humorist Bradley Sands returns with one of the strangest, most hilarious collections of the year. **130 pages $11**

BB-106 "Mr. Magic Realism" Bruce Taylor—Like Golden Age science fiction comics written by Freud, *Mr. Magic Realism* is a strange, insightful adventure that spans the furthest reaches of the galaxy, exploring the hidden caverns in the hearts and minds of men, women, aliens, and biomechanical cats. **152 pages $11**

BB-107 **"Zombies and Shit" Carlton Mellick III**—"Battle Royale" meets "Return of the Living Dead." Mellick's bizarro tribute to the zombie genre. **308 pages $13**

BB-108 **"The Cannibal's Guide to Ethical Living" Mykle Hansen**— Over a five star French meal of fine wine, organic vegetables and human flesh, a lunatic delivers a witty, chilling, disturbingly sane argument in favor of eating the rich.. **184 pages $11**

BB-109 **"Starfish Girl" Athena Villaverde**—In a post-apocalyptic underwater dome society, a girl with a starfish growing from her head and an assassin with sea anenome hair are on the run from a gang of mutant fish men. **160 pages $11**

BB-110 **"Lick Your Neighbor" Chris Genoa**—Mutant ninjas, a talking whale, kung fu masters, maniacal pilgrims, and an alcoholic clown populate Chris Genoa's surreal, darkly comical and unnerving reimagining of the first Thanksgiving. **303 pages $13**

BB-111 **"Night of the Assholes" Kevin L. Donihe**—A plague of assholes is infecting the countryside. Normal everyday people are transforming into jerks, snobs, dicks, and douchebags. And they all have only one purpose: to make your life a living hell.. **192 pages $11**

BB-112 **"Jimmy Plush, Teddy Bear Detective" Garrett Cook**—Hardboiled cases of a private detective trapped within a teddy bear body. **180 pages $11**

BB-113 **"The Deadheart Shelters" Forrest Armstrong**—The hip hop lovechild of William Burroughs and Dali... **144 pages $11**

BB-114 **"Eyeballs Growing All Over Me... Again" Tony Raugh**— Absurd, surreal, playful, dream-like, whimsical, and a lot of fun to read. **144 pages $11**

BB-115 **"Whargoul" Dave Brockie** — From the killing grounds of Stalingrad to the death camps of the holocaust. From torture chambers in Iraq to race riots in the United States, the Whargoul was there, killing and raping. **244 pages $12**

BB-116 **"By the Time We Leave Here, We'll Be Friends" J. David Osborne** — A David Lynchian nightmare set in a Russian gulag, where its prisoners, guards, traitors, soldiers, lovers, and demons fight for survival and their own rapidly deteriorating humanity. **168 pages $11**

BB-117 **"Christmas on Crack" edited by Carlton Mellick III** — Perverted Christmas Tales for the whole family! . . . as long as every member of your family is over the age of 18. **168 pages $11**

BB-118 **"Crab Town" Carlton Mellick III** — Radiation fetishists, balloon people, mutant crabs, sail-bike road warriors, and a love affair between a woman and an H-Bomb. This is one mean asshole of a city. Welcome to Crab Town. **100 pages $8**

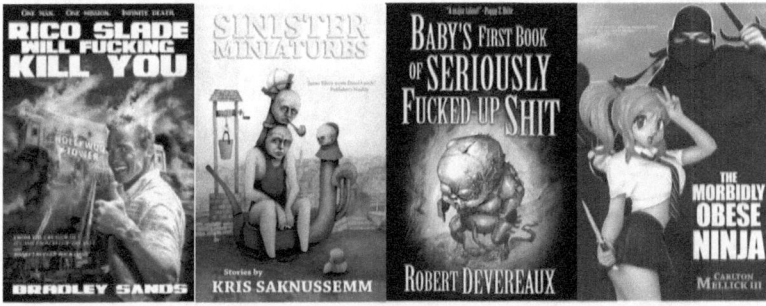

BB-119 **"Rico Slade Will Fucking Kill You" Bradley Sands** — Rico Slade is an action hero. Rico Slade can rip out a throat with his bare hands. Rico Slade's favorite food is the honey-roasted peanut. Rico Slade will fucking kill everyone. A novel. **122 pages $8**

BB-120 **"Sinister Miniatures" Kris Saknussemm** — The definitive collection of short fiction by Kris Saknussemm, confirming that he is one of the best, most daring writers of the weird to emerge in the twenty-first century. **180 pages $11**

BB-121 **"Baby's First Book of Seriously Fucked up Shit" Robert Devereaux** — Ten stories of the strange, the gross, and the just plain fucked up from one of the most original voices in horror. **176 pages $11**

BB-122 **"The Morbidly Obese Ninja" Carlton Mellick III** — These days, if you want to run a successful company . . . you're going to need a lot of ninjas. **92 pages $8**

BB-123 **"Abortion Arcade" Cameron Pierce** — An intoxicating blend of body horror and midnight movie madness, reminiscent of early David Lynch and the splatterpunks at their most sublime. **172 pages $11**

BB-124 **"Black Hole Blues" Patrick Wensink** — A hilarious double helix of country music and physics. **196 pages $11**

BB-125 **"Barbarian Beast Bitches of the Badlands" Carlton Mellick III** — Three prequels and sequels to *Warrior Wolf Women of the Wasteland.* **284 pages $13**

BB-126 **"The Traveling Dildo Salesman" Kevin L. Donihe** — A nightmare comedy about destiny, faith, and sex toys. Also featuring Donihe's most lurid and infamous short stories: *Milky Agitation, Two-Way Santa, The Helen Mower, Living Room Zombies,* and *Revenge of the Living Masturbation Rag.* **108 pages $8**

BB-127 **"Metamorphosis Blues" Bruce Taylor** — Enter a land of love beasts, intergalactic cowboys, and rock 'n roll. A land where Sears Catalogs are doorways to insanity and men keep mysterious black boxes. Welcome to the monstrous mind of Mr. Magic Realism. **136 pages $11**

BB-128 **"The Driver's Guide to Hitting Pedestrians" Andersen Prunty** — A pocket guide to the twenty-three most painful things in life, written by the most well-adjusted man in the universe. **108 pages $8**

BB-129 **"Island of the Super People" Kevin Shamel** — Four students and their anthropology professor journey to a remote island to study its indigenous population. But this is no ordinary native culture. They're super heroes and villains with flesh costumes and out-landish abilities like self-detonation, musical eyelashes, and microwave hands. **194 pages $11**

BB-130 **"Fantastic Orgy" Carlton Mellick III** — Shark Sex, mutant cats, and strange sexually transmitted diseases. Featuring the stories: *Candy-coated, Ear Cat, Fantastic Orgy, City Hobgoblins,* and *Porno in August.* **136 pages $9**

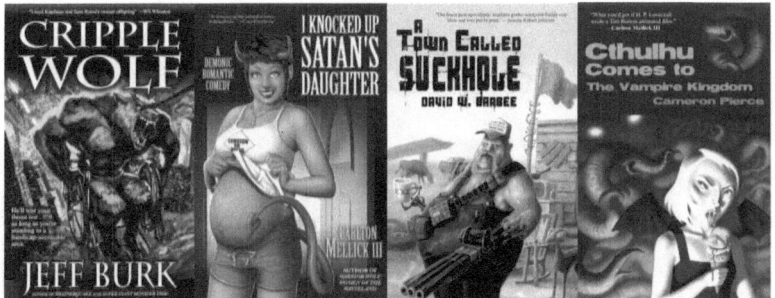

BB-131 "Cripple Wolf" Jeff Burk — Part man. Part wolf. 100% crippled. Also including *Punk Rock Nursing Home, Adrift with Space Badgers, Cook for Your Life, Just Another Day in the Park, Frosty and the Full Monty*, and *House of Cats*. **152 pages $10**

BB-132 "I Knocked Up Satan's Daughter" Carlton Mellick III — An adorable, violent, fantastical love story. A romantic comedy for the bizarro fiction reader. **152 pages $10**

BB-133 "A Town Called Suckhole" David W. Barbee — Far into the future, in the nuclear bowels of post-apocalyptic Dixie, there is a town. A town of derelict mobile homes, ancient junk, and mutant wildlife. A town of slack jawed rednecks who bask in the splendors of moonshine and mud boggin'. A town dedicated to the bloody and demented legacy of the Old South. A town called Suckhole. **144 pages $10**

BB-134 "Cthulhu Comes to the Vampire Kingdom" Cameron Pierce — What you'd get if H. P. Lovecraft wrote a Tim Burton animated film. **148 pages $11**

BB-135 "I am Genghis Cum" Violet LeVoit — From the savage Arctic tundra to post-partum mutations to your missing daughter's unmarked grave, join visionary madwoman Violet LeVoit in this non-stop eight-story onslaught of full-tilt Bizarro punk lit thrills. **124 pages $9**

BB-136 "Haunt" Laura Lee Bahr — A tripping-balls Los Angeles noir, where a mysterious dame drags you through a time-warping Bizarro hall of mirrors. **316 pages $13**

BB-137 "Amazing Stories of the Flying Spaghetti Monster" edited by Cameron Pierce — Like an all-spaghetti evening of Adult Swim, the Flying Spaghetti Monster will show you the many realms of His Noodly Appendage. Learn of those who worship him and the lives he touches in distant, mysterious ways. **228 pages $12**

BB-138 "Wave of Mutilation" Douglas Lain — A dream-pop exploration of modern architecture and the American identity, *Wave of Mutilation* is a Zen finger trap for the 21st century. **100 pages $8**

BB-139 **"Hooray for Death!" Mykle Hansen** — Famous Author Mykle Hansen draws unconventional humor from deaths tiny and large, and invites you to laugh while you can. **128 pages $10**

BB-140 **"Hypno-hog's Moonshine Monster Jamboree" Andrew Goldfarb** — Hicks, Hogs, Horror! Goldfarb is back with another strange illustrated tale of backwoods weirdness. **120 pages $9**

BB-141 **"Broken Piano For President" Patrick Wensink** — A comic masterpiece about the fast food industry, booze, and the necessity to choose happiness over work and security. **372 pages $15**

BB-142 **"Please Do Not Shoot Me in the Face" Bradley Sands** — A novel in three parts, *Please Do Not Shoot Me in the Face: A Novel*, is the story of one boy detective, the worst ninja in the world, and the great American fast food wars. It is a novel of loss, destruction, and--incredibly--genuine hope. **224 pages $12**

BB-143 **"Santa Steps Out" Robert Devereaux** — Sex, Death, and Santa Claus ... The ultimate erotic Christmas story is back. **294 pages $13**

BB-144 **"Santa Conquers the Homophobes" Robert Devereaux** — "I wish I could hope to ever attain one-thousandth the perversity of Robert Devereaux's toenail clippings." - Poppy Z. Brite **316 pages $13**

BB-145 **"We Live Inside You" Jeremy Robert Johnson** — "Jeremy Robert Johnson is dancing to a way different drummer. He loves language, he loves the edge, and he loves us people. These stories have range and style and wit. This is entertainment... and literature."- Jack Ketchum **188 pages $11**

BB-146 **"Clockwork Girl" Athena Villaverde** — Urban fairy tales for the weird girl in all of us. Like a combination of Francesca Lia Block, Charles de Lint, Kathe Koja, Tim Burton, and Hayao Miyazaki, her stories are cute, kinky, edgy, magical, provocative, and strange, full of poetic imagery and vicious sexuality. **160 pages $10**

BB-147 **"Armadillo Fists" Carlton Mellick III** — A weird-as-hell gangster story set in a world where people drive giant mechanical dinosaurs instead of cars. **168 pages $11**

BB-148 **"Gargoyle Girls of Spider Island" Cameron Pierce** — Four college seniors venture out into open waters for the tropical party weekend of a lifetime. Instead of a teenage sex fantasy, they find themselves in a nightmare of pirates, sharks, and sex-crazed monsters. **100 pages $8**

BB-149 **"The Handsome Squirm" by Carlton Mellick III** — Like Franz Kafka's *The Trial* meets an erotic body horror version of *The Blob.* **158 pages $11**

BB-150 **"Tentacle Death Trip" Jordan Krall** — It's *Death Race 2000* meets H. P. Lovecraft in bizarro author Jordan Krall's best and most suspenseful work to date. **224 pages $12**

BB-151 **"The Obese" Nick Antosca** — Like Alfred Hitchcock's *The Birds*... but with obese people. **108 pages $10**

BB-152 **"All-Monster Action!" Cody Goodfellow** — The world gave him a blank check and a demand: Create giant monsters to fight our wars. But Dr. Otaku was not satisfied with mere chaos and mass destruction.... **216 pages $12**

BB-153 **"Ugly Heaven" Carlton Mellick III** — Heaven is no longer a paradise. It was once a blissful utopia full of wonders far beyond human comprehension. But the afterlife is now in ruins. It has become an ugly, lonely wasteland populated by strange monstrous beasts, masturbating angels, and sad man-like beings wallowing in the remains of the once-great Kingdom of God. **106 pages $8**

BB-154 **"Space Walrus" Kevin L. Donihe** — Walter is supposed to go where no walrus has ever gone before, but all this astronaut walrus really wants is to take it easy on the intense training, escape the chimpanzee bullies, and win the love of his human trainer Dr. Stephanie. **160 pages $11**